"PERHAPS YOU HAVE ME MEMORIZED . . ."

A teasing smile played across her lips as she looked at him questioningly.

"I'm afraid you don't understand," he said. "The dress is only complementary to the pictures and may not in the end be very important. I'm studying your face . . . and a face like yours could be studied for a thousand years and never completely memorized, because it changes from moment to moment. I can only hope to capture the moment that seems the most like you."

"That sounds quite difficult to me," she said, contemplating his words with a frown. "Capturing a moment, I mean." She turned to regard this man whom she had come to respect, wondering whether to open her private world to him. Finally she spoke. "Do you . . . what do you think of eternity?"

He looked at her sharply, aware that this was no trivial question. "That's a big one," he admitted softly. "But just as your face cannot be memorized, God's ways can never be totally understood. "But I know that God is in control of eternity and, though I may buck and storm, in the end I'm glad He's in charge."

"And you're not afraid to die?"

"Everyone's afraid to die, I guess. No one knows just what it will be like and that scares us. But there's no need to ruin the heaven on this side and the other side of the bridge of death worrying about whether the planks will hold."

She stole a glance at his face, visible above the back of the easel. His heavy brows were furrowed in deep concentration, his mouth set in a firm line. *Even when he is grim, he is so very handsome,* she thought and then wondered why he had never married.

JULIANA OF CLOVER HILL

Brenda Knight Graham

of the Zondervan Publishing House
Grand Rapids, Michigan

This book is based on a true story, but the names of the characters, with the exception of one or two, have been changed.

JULIANA OF CLOVER HILL

1415 Lake Drive, S.E.,
Grand Rapids, Michigan 49506

Library of Congress Cataloging in Publication Data

Graham, Brenda Knight.
Juliana of Clover Hill.

I. Title.
PS3557.R185J8 1984 813'.54 83-19776
ISBN 0-310-46422-6

Edited by Anne Severance
Designed by Kim Koning

Printed in the United States of America

85 86 87 88 89 / 8 7 6 5 4 3

This book is lovingly dedicated
to the memory of
my father
F. S. Knight

ACKNOWLEDGMENTS

I hesitate to make any written acknowledgments for fear I will leave someone out, but I hesitate even more to make no acknowledgments when certain ones have helped so much to make this book possible.

My husband, Charles Graham, must be at the head of this list because of his all-round patience, encouragement, and enthusiasm. My mother, Eula Gibbs Knight, was my main source of information. She never once exclaimed, "You already asked me that!" or "Can't you just leave me alone!" I would like to say a special thanks, too, to my children, William and Julie, for their understanding.

Burns Gibbs, the late Hugh Gibbs, and Emma Berrong gave invaluable help contributing to the background information. Hamilton Gibbs kindly allowed me free range on Clover Hill which he now owns. Stanley Knight, Pat Peck and Jackie Eastham gave me much constructive criticism. Revonda and Marcus Barwick saved my sanity by arranging a secluded spot where I could type, uninterrupted by the telephone.

Helping me with a background reading list were Barbara Williams and her daughter Linda Kay of Cairo's Roddenbery Memorial Library. I appreciate also the help of Virginia Tyre of The Northeast Georgia Regional Library in Clarkesville, Georgia and Darrell Terrell of Kent State University.

Lastly, I must say thanks to my friend Ruth Davis who took over another assignment so that I could be free to spend time on *Juliana*.

CHAPTER 1

JULIANA COULD TELL BY THE tracks in the mud, even before she pulled open the mailbox door, that the mail carrier had finally come. Since he'd started driving a car instead of his faithful horse, one could never be sure when he would arrive. Henry, Juliana's farmer brother, wanted a tractor, but not a car. Even now in 1919, when so many people owned cars that they were demanding the roads be improved so they wouldn't have to dart around treacherous wagon ruts, Henry still said he preferred his horse Maude with her sensitive response to his every word. Juliana smiled as she stepped across the ribby track. She would rather have Maude, too; she didn't make nearly as much noise.

As she pulled out the mail, being careful to keep it secure in the roll of Papa's paper so nothing would fall in the mud, she could hear again as if she weren't half a mile away now, Mamma saying, "Juliana, why *must* you go for the mail now before dinner? What are you expecting?"

What, indeed, was she expecting? How could she explain that she had no earthly idea—that she was just expecting Something to Happen. At fifteen her whole body ached with awareness—the songs of wood thrush, warbler, and mockingbird, the stirring of a warm breeze that dipped up under her wide hat and brushed her hot cheeks, the crackling of seed pods exploding in the August heat along the roadside, the steamy green smell of last night's rain evaporating from dogwood, pine, and rich acres of corn. Sometimes she wished intensely to know what she was expecting, what was out there beyond hoeing corn, feeding chickens, churning, scrubbing floors on Saturday, and going to church on Sunday. At other times it simply didn't matter; knowing there *was* Something was enough.

Juliana skillfully avoided all the mud puddles, though her eyes seemed wholly occupied with studying each piece of mail. She hefted a letter from Richard's wife Frances to Mamma—a stiff thick letter. Perhaps it had a picture of Baby Jack in it. Of her three nieces and nephews, Baby Jack was the youngest and nearest, living in Clarkesville where her brother Richard was a banker. There was a post card from Brother in his own scratchy handwriting. His name was Calvin, but everyone, including Mamma, called him Brother. He liked his church in Nacoochee and was looking forward to teaching as well as preaching when school began in the fall. His wife Winnie and the two children were fine.

She stopped to look at the next one addressed to Mrs. Grange Neal. Why, oh, why had Grange married Molly? She might not be so dull and boring if she weren't always sick, but she was always sick. That's why she was spending the summer at Clover Hill while Grange worked in Atlanta. Mamma had said if Papa were still here, he would want them all to care for Grange's sick wife. Anyway, Mama herself would never turn down an opportunity to help someone. In the case of Molly, Juliana couldn't help wishing sometimes that Mamma wasn't so soft-hearted.

It was not that she was jealous of Molly, for, after all, Grange was much too old for Juliana to consider romantically. He must be at least twenty-five by now! No, it was just that Grange was a special friend of the whole family, and it was disappointing to see him tied to someone so unimaginative. Oh, Grange wasn't sorry for himself. One would never know he was unhappy by the way he joked and teased, but she knew he must be.

Her lips curved up in a gentle smile in the shadow of her hat as she remembered the first present Grange had given her: blue hair ribbons to wear for her first day of school in Cornelia. "To match your eyes," he'd said, giving her hair a teasing jerk. She looked at her hair now where it had fallen forward down over her calico dress, and she pushed the blond masses back over her shoulder with one hand as she walked on.

She rubbed her finger back and forth over Papa's name on the paper, thinking how strange that Papa was not here anymore, that the Atlanta Constitution still came to L. B. Hamilton, though he was over in

Level Grove Cemetery. It seemed so unfair that the essence of Papa was gone—his commanding voice, the rough hands that ran the sawmill and brought Mamma the first clump of violets in the spring, his lively interest in all that was happening in the world—while the house he had built and the dairy and the fields he had plowed were still here.

While thousands were dying as victims of the war or flu, Papa died with an ulcerated stomach. He kept on working at the farm, optimistically expecting good news from Europe, until a short week before he died. Then, in October, with the churches and schools officially closed as the flu epidemic took its toll, he was buried in the cemetery. Mamma said she believed Papa knew that Henry came home safely without being sent to Europe and that Papa was alive in heaven, not in the cemetery.

Juliana glanced ahead at the shafts of sunshine falling through the trees, glancing off the puddles in the road, shifting between leafy shadows in front of her—lively, reaching, *touching* sunshine. Was Papa still somewhere? She could say she believed with Mamma, but down deep inside she wasn't at all sure.

The war itself had been no worse than the flu epidemic, which had taken one from nearly every family in their small church. She still shuddered at the memory of seeing Sister so sick, of the small children whom Mamma bathed and prepared for burial, of the day when even Mamma herself had become deathly ill. There had been times when she and her next older brother Byron had not known whether anyone else in the family would survive. They had worked side by side at Clover Hill, even hauling hay all one night to keep the rain from spoiling it. There had been no Christmas that year. Only she and Byron were well enough to do anything, and they had baked a cake. But because of the sugar rationing, it had to be made with honey. There weren't enough eggs or butter, either, because of all they were required to turn in for government use. It took every shred of imagination to make that cake palatable.

Maybe it was because of the dread and horror of last year that this year was so full of life until her fingertips even tingled with excitement over absolutely nothing. The prospect of school in September was challenging, yet she felt she could never be happier than when she was roaming the woods and pastures of Clover Hill. To find a tiger lily blooming in an opening between the pines, like a queen in her throne room, was a big event. But there was something much, much bigger coming somehow—and soon—even though the mail held no hint of what it might be.

Hearing Byron call her name, she suddenly remembered Mamma was waiting dinner for her. Like a deer newly aware of curious onlookers invading its private world, she sped along the winding woods road, arriving at the porch steps out of breath, her cheeks pink with heat and exertion.

Molly was rocking on the porch, just barely pushing her thick body enough to make the straw-bottomed rocker squeak. She hardly even blinked as Juliana dropped Grange's letter in her lap.

"Come now, dinner is ready. Whatever took you so long?" asked Sister as Juliana hung her hat on a nail by the door. Sister, whose real name was Emily, understood many things, but she couldn't understand anyone's being late for dinner unless the cows were out or the barn was on fire.

"Just—looking," answered Juliana.

"Well, it's most upsetting. There was Byron supposed to be cleaning the barn, but reading a book instead, and Henry taking his own long time coming in from the field. At least we should only have to wait on the men. There's no excuse for you. . . ."

"Now, now, Sister," said Mamma. "We're all here, except—Molly," she directed her voice through the screen door. "Please come to dinner, Molly. You can read your letter afterwards. It'll keep."

Mamma calmly eased herself into her chair, letting out a little sigh of relief for the chance to rest a minute. Then, seeing Sister impatiently pacing, she smiled and motioned her to sit down, too. "No use fuming, Sister," she said, the tiny wrinkles crinkling around her eyes.

Juliana ran some water into the wash bowl in the kitchen and bathed her face, delighting in the coolness of the well water. She knew she had plenty of time to wash up while Molly lumbered to the table. But Sister called out in exasperation. "Juliana! Do come on! You're going to spend half your life primping and preening."

"Oh, leave her alone," said Henry, already seated in Papa's chair at the table. "Sister, you're so insistent that women should be allowed to vote, but you're not being fair to the women in your own household."

Sister's only answer was a quick glance as she

tucked a stray strand of hair behind her ear and bit her lip.

"Come now, everyone," said Mamma. "Help Molly with her chair, Byron."

Whether it was Byron's face peering solemnly over the top of Molly's head, or the way Molly grabbed a biscuit the instant she was seated as if they might all disappear, or whether the tension-filled atmosphere demanded release, when Juliana caught Sister's eye, the two of them seemed to explode with laughter, all ill will forgotten between them.

It had always been so during mealtime at Clover Hill: either Sister and Byron, or Sister and Juliana, or all three going into spasms of giggling. There had been times when Papa had even sent them outside until they could gain control. Not that he was against laughing, but he did not feel the place for hysterics was at the dinner table. Even now it was the memory of Papa's stern blue gaze that caused the girls to choke down their giggles as Henry bowed his head over his gripped brown hands and said grace.

Henry had come back from his stint in the army sobered, thin, and white from a long siege of the dreaded flu. He had tackled the farm work courageously as Papa had trained him to do. Juliana, the faithful water girl, had come upon him muttering to the horses. She knew then he had wanted to go out west, that he had even been bitterly disappointed when the flu kept him from being shipped to Europe. She knew that he shared her love of Clover Hill, yet felt imprisoned by it.

Since eighth grade he had stayed home to work the

farm rather than go to school with the others. Whether it was because he was exceptionally adept with tools and horses, or because the other boys were exceptionally good at their books, it was hard to say. Anyway, he'd always said one of them had to stay at home and work. Fair or not, Henry was chosen. Mamma had pled for him at times, but it had done no good. As determined as Papa was that the others stay in school and learn every bit they could, he was just as determined that Henry should be the farmer. "There has to be one in every family," he said. "Take away the farm, and how will the nation eat?"

Clover Hill House, set among a stand of oaks, was shaped like an ell instead of being square as most farmhouses were. Juliana was glad it was different. Actually the house had somehow grown with the family, as Burns Hamilton could spare lumber from his mill and time from his farming and thinking up new inventions. The first little two-room house was on the property when Burns came to take over the farm from his father. Instead of building onto it, he had built another two-room house beside the first.

Finally, one summer, he had connected them with two more rooms in the middle. Mamma was in Commerce at that time, nursing Byron after an appendectomy. Juliana remembered how Papa and the boys had worked from dawn till dark to finish the rooms before Mamma came home. He was so proud to show her the new addition he almost snapped his suspenders.

Each room, except the kitchen, had been used at one time as a bedroom. The house was adequate, if not spacious, for raising six children. Mamma had hooked rugs, crocheted and tatted bedspreads and chair throws—beautiful things that could have graced the governor's mansion. She had always been proud of the hardwood floors, standing back after a weekly scrubbing to admire them and say, "Thank God for pretty windows and floors." It didn't matter that the level of the three sets of floors didn't quite meet. That gave the house character. Though she must have been exasperated at times with Papa's zeal for creating inventions that somehow never made it to the patent office, Mamma always displayed only pride in being married to the man who was the first to grow winter grass in Habersham County, Georgia.

After dinner Henry stayed at the table reading the *Constitution,* now and then commenting on the news. Mamma read her letter and card out loud to them, while Molly labored over her own letter. Juliana squirmed, wishing she could grab it and find out quickly what Grange had said. Just as she and Sister were beginning to stack the heavy white plates, Molly commented as if it were everyday news, "Grange wants Byron to go with us over to Clarkesville for Sunday dinner."

"Sunday dinner?" asked Mamma, suddenly curious.

"With Mr. Kirk and his old maid aunt."

"Don't you think *spinster* sounds better, Molly? Anyway, who is Mr. Kirk?"

"You don't know?" Molly raised her eyebrows in as much surprise as she ever showed.

"No," said Mamma.

"He's an artist." Molly reached for another biscuit

and leaned back to eat it, spilling crumbs in her lap.

"What kind of artist?" asked Mamma.

Molly finished the biscuit and dusted crumbs onto the floor before she answered. "A proud one." She said, "Every girl in Atlanta would like to marry him, but I never saw what they liked about him. He may be good-looking and tall, but he is—well, he's stuck up."

"I think Mamma meant what kind of pictures does he paint," smiled Sister, threatening to burst into giggles again.

"Oh—that. He does pictures of mountains, waterfalls, trees. Grange seems to think Byron would like to see them."

"Grange has always been so thoughtful. Well, Byron, what do you think?" asked Mamma.

Byron seemed even younger than his seventeen years when he looked up from studying his fork as if he'd never seen it before. "I appreciate the invitation, but I couldn't go—that is, not unless Juliana goes, too," he stumbled.

"But I—" began Juliana, then stopped as she recognized her brother's pleading look. The two of them had always shared personal problems, and she realized it was Byron's innate shyness that was behind the invitation, not his overwhelming desire for her to meet the artist, too. "I would like to go," she said, watching Molly's face for her reaction. She looked at Juliana quickly, a look of wariness in her eyes, as if a hidden thought had been discovered and exposed.

"Only Byron was invited," said Molly bluntly.

"That's true. So only Byron will go," said

Mamma, standing up and pushing her chair to the table. "Grange knows Byron is very interested in poetry and art."

"But I am, too," said Juliana impulsively, and then blushed as Mamma gave her a hard look. She hadn't meant to beg. She was only trying to help Byron out.

"I don't think either of you needs to go," said Henry, laying his paper down and pushing his chair back. "Neither one of you ought to miss church."

"But, Henry, you said yourself we depend too much on ritual," said Sister. "This would be an opportunity for Byron to broaden his horizons."

"If Byron has already decided to be a minister, then he need not consider the arts."

"Henry, how very narrow-minded of you!" said Sister, her face reddening.

"I didn't make the decision—he did," said Henry, taking his hat from its nail as he started out the door.

"You know that's not what I mean!"

Henry grinned, shrugged his shoulders, and walked out. "Oh, that boy!" exclaimed Sister, twisting a tea cloth in her hands until Mamma calmly took it from her and smoothed it out on the table.

From Wednesday until Friday the subject of visiting the artist was discussed and rediscussed until Juliana had developed a great interest in seeing him for herself, not just on Byron's account. She was very curious about this Mr. Kirk for whom, Molly said, girls primped for hours, only to have him pay them no heed at all. "A proud man," Molly kept saying. "Talented, but, oh so proud!"

On Friday Grange came, and, in only a few minutes

punctuated with explosions of his deep laughter, he had convinced Mamma that both the young people should make the trip. "I've met Foster's Aunt De and I'm quite sure she won't mind having Juliana along."

"But isn't there a phone? Couldn't we call and ask?"

Grange threw back his head and laughed heartily. "A phone? Foster Kirk with a phone! It would be preposterous. Mamma Hamilton, you don't seem to understand. Foster Kirk is a real artist and one I predict will become famous nationwide one day. But like other artists he only welcomes intrusion when he asks for it. A telephone! Never!"

"But what is he really like, Grange?"

"Oh, you have nothing to worry about concerning his character."

"But you said he was like other artists, and—well, I've heard so much . . ."

"Foster Kirk has been called stuck-up because he won't even accept a social drink."

"Grange, if you don't mind my asking," said Henry, "just how did you meet this man? I know you like art and music, but . . ."

"I met him in a men's Sunday school class. He and I had the reputation for being—what shall I say?—troublemakers. Because we asked too many questions, probably. Actually, I think Mr. Keller, our teacher, really welcomed our—discussions. Otherwise, Foster would have certainly found another class."

"In other words, you argued," said Henry, an amused smile playing on his lips.

"Some would call it that. We called it questioning

before belief. I will say this about Foster,'' said Grange, stretching out his lanky legs and clasping his hands behind his head. ''Foster has a much harder head than I, yet a keen sensitivity to go along with it. He would no more accept a statement without challenging its truth than he would attempt to capture on his canvas something he had not seen. Truth is the guiding force of his life.''

Juliana, her chin cupped in her hands, listened with interest, her eyes fastened on Grange's face. She was eager to glean every bit of information she could about this stranger she was soon to meet.

From under half-closed eyelids, Molly was watching Juliana.

CHAPTER 2

MOLLY'S EYES LOOKED somber, Juliana thought, as they started out that Sunday morning. For one beginning a rare outing, she didn't look very happy, even though she had Grange at her side.

Henry complained as he drove them in the surrey to meet the train. "Shouldn't be traveling on Sunday. Could have picked some other day if you had to go on such a jaunt." But just the same he lifted his hat as they boarded the train, a sign of grudging good will.

Byron and Juliana sat together in the train, across the aisle from Grange and Molly. The car was full of people going to Tallulah Falls for the day. At least that's where Juliana assumed they were going in their pretty straw hats with their picnic baskets at their feet. It was a popular place with Atlanta people in the summer. If they had been going to Clarkesville to stay in one of the hotels or to Tiger to spend the summer in one of the quaint little mountain cottages, they would have their suitcases with them. Tallulah Falls drew hundreds of people just to spend a few hours viewing the spectacular gorge that some, who had seen both, said was prettier than the Grand Canyon.

Clarkesville had two fine hotels, one of which Clover Hill had supplied with milk back when it had been a thriving dairy instead of an all-around farm as it was now, with apples as its main cash crop. Juliana remembered riding with Richard to deliver milk once when she was quite small. The only other time she had been to Clarkesville was when Papa had brought the whole family to the "A and M School" to see a farm exhibit. It had been an all-day excursion with the most significant memory for Juliana being the model of a farm with tiny horses, little houses and barn, wagons, even detailed miniature plows and bales of hay. Papa had spent all his time looking at a tractor and then had talked all the way home about what it could do.

"We won't go into Clarkesville," said Grange, leaning across the aisle to speak to Byron. "We stop at Hill's Crossing on the other side of town. It's a stone's throw from the back of Foster Kirk's place."

"How far is it now?" asked Juliana.

Grange looked out the window, then pulled his watch out of his pocket. "I'd say maybe seven minutes—depending on how long we're held up at the Clarkesville station."

"That close?" asked Byron.

Grange laughed and slapped Byron on the arm. "Now, Byron, loosen up, old boy. Foster Kirk is just a plain guy. He'll expect no fancy talk."

"What about talk of any kind?" whispered Byron to Juliana.

"Maybe we could just forget to get off and go on to Tallulah Falls for the day," said Juliana wistfully, picking at the eyelet ruffle on a puffed sleeve of her blue gingham dress. She knew as well as Byron that they must be nice to Grange's friends, but nothing would have pleased them more than to be allowed to go on to Tallulah.

The stop in Clarkesville was not long enough and shortly Grange was getting up, helping Molly out of her seat, and saying cheerfully, "Come on, troops, this is it."

In a sudden panic Juliana wondered why she had ever agreed to accompany Byron. Byron could have just stayed at home if he were too shy to visit without her. Suppose she really wasn't welcome? How utterly embarrassing it would be!

As they went down the steps, Byron pushing her ahead of him—not solely from gentlemanly behavior—she caught a glimpse of the man who must be Foster Kirk. He was squeezing Grange's hand and smiling at Molly. She had time to notice that he was tall and dressed in neat khakis.

Then, as Grange said something to him, Mr. Kirk glanced up at her. For a moment her heart seemed to stop completely. She lost awareness of the conductor's hand under her elbow, of the buzzing crowd of passengers, of Grange and Molly looking up at her quizzically, of Byron crushing the brim of his hat in his hands behind her. Foster Kirk's eyes held hers for an eternal moment—laughing, serious, questioning eyes.

She could not look away. If it were possible for someone to scowl and smile at the same time, he was doing it, and his dark mustache twitched just slightly. Why did it seem as if she'd seen him before, and as if he were teasing her about it?

Then, like frozen characters come back to life, everyone was real again. Pink and flustered, Juliana lowered her eyes under her blue straw hat and watched her own feet carefully as she stepped to the ground.

As the train puffed away, Foster Kirk directed them to a small path through a field of broom sedge. "It will be cool when we reach the shade of the trees," he assured them, observing how Molly was already panting.

"I do hope you don't mind our bringing Juliana along," said Molly between puffs. "She so wanted to come. I didn't think it was a good idea, but . . ."

"It was a very good idea," said Mr. Kirk. "My aunt will be delighted. She has an enormous meal prepared."

He spoke so positively that Molly could say no more. Byron nudged Juliana's arm and grinned at her. "Poor Molly," he whispered in mock sadness.

It was cooler in the woods as Mr. Kirk had promised, and the brother and sister bringing up the rear of the little parade took time to observe everything—a vireo's nest hung like a tiny hammock between twigs of a dogwood tree, an array of bright orange flowers that reminded Juliana of mounds of grated carrot when Mamma was making carrot pudding, small huckleberry bushes with a stray berry or two still clinging to them, and all along the trail, tall pines under which stretched a thick carpet of brown needles.

"My mother named the place Pinedale," Mr. Kirk was saying. "Though this isn't part of the original homestead, it's very like it. Many, many pines. And here is where I'd like to build a home someday," he said, stopping and directing their attention with a wave of his hand to an opening in the timber on top of a hill. One could see mountains in two different directions. Juliana spied a tiny maple with protective stakes around it.

"It's about time you let us rest," gasped Molly, hanging on Grange's arm. "You and your long legs will have us all exhausted."

Mr. Kirk didn't even seem to notice Molly. "From here you can see Trey Mountain to the northwest and Yonah to the west. I've been keeping the trees trimmed so these views would stay open. I think it's almost as important what you can see from a house as what the house is like itself. But there is good clay here, too, with underlying rock—a solid foundation."

"You sound as if you have plans," said Grange.

"I always have plans," said Mr. Kirk with a laugh. "Not that they always work out."

"It truly is beautiful," breathed Byron, and Juliana knew he was finally glad he'd come. Her own lips parted in pleasure at the view of the distant blue mountains speared by nearby pine. The blue was like no other blue she had ever seen. Not like robins' eggs or the bluest of asters or forget-me-nots. Not even like the sky.

"Well, come now," said Mr. Kirk briskly, starting down the hill. "The two little houses you'll see in a minute are part of the original homestead. The smaller one was built in 1888 by my father, and the other one later, as he needed to divide his own growing family from his in-laws. I use the little one now for my studio, and Aunt De keeps the cottage going."

"Foster, did you ever tell us what happened to your mother?" asked Molly.

Juliana was suddenly aware of the muffled sound of their footsteps on the pine needles, and of the clear distinct call of a mourning dove. Ahead of her she saw Mr. Kirk's hands clenched together behind him. After a bit he replied, his words clipped, "My mother died of tuberculosis when I was thirteen."

"And your father?"

"Molly—really, dear," began Grange.

"It's all right, Grange. My father and sister live in Chicago."

"But wouldn't that be a good place for an artist to live, too?"

Again there was a pause. Molly's labored breathing sounded like the horses after they'd plowed Long Bottom all morning. Juliana wished she would just breathe and stop giving her third-degree examination, although she herself listened closely for the answer.

"It would be a good place to live, I suppose, if that were where one wanted to live. I lived there while I attended the art institute. But for me there could never be any place but Pinedale. And I could spend the rest of my days here and barely scratch the surface of all the subjects there are to paint."

As they came in sight of the quaint gray buildings, nestled in a valley not much bigger than the houses themselves, Juliana had another seizure of panic. Now she must meet the aunt who was not expecting her and might well resent her presence at the dinner table. There was smoke rising from the chimney of the larger house where they would be eating. She prayed fervently that there would not be fried chicken or anything messy. She could see herself with an awkward piece of chicken in her lap and the laughing eyes of this inquisitive artist fixed on her.

Miss Delia Sweet was tall, angular, her lips thinly pressed into a polite smile, her hand hard and cool as she shook Juliana's sweaty one. Juliana could not be at all sure she didn't mind the extra guest, even though there certainly was plenty to eat.

But there was no fried chicken. Instead, there was beef roast sliced so thin you could almost see through it—if it weren't drowned in the most delicious brown gravy Juliana had ever tasted. There were potatoes cooked in a white sauce, and green beans that were a pretty color, but didn't taste like Mamma's, which she simmered for hours with a chunk of hog jowl.

Everything was served on thin china bordered with a delicate wreath of flowers, nothing like the thick practical dishes at Clover Hill. But Juliana noticed, too, the many chips on the edges and the tiny dark cracks sprayed out in all directions like granny faces.

However, there was one very distasteful dish. When Molly passed Juliana a bowl containing something brown and slimy-looking, she took only a tiny portion. Miss Sweet noticed her doubtful expression and exclaimed, "The child has never eaten mushrooms! Come now, take more than that." She reached across

Byron to spoon more onto her plate. It was all Juliana could do to eat the slick slices that reminded her of garden slugs cut into bite-sized pieces. Byron whispered to her once that he would eat them, that they were really good, but she felt Miss Sweet's eyes on her and, oddly, she was determined to eat those mushrooms, no matter what.

As she ate she felt a cat rub against her legs, then another and another. Her curiosity finally got the best of her and she looked under the table, counting quickly four—no, five—cats. She wanted very much to ask how many cats belonged to this household, but everyone was involved in a conversation about Woodrow Wilson's dreams for the League of Nations. Even Byron was talking now. All that reading he'd done was paying off, and he was sounding every bit as informed as the older men. Juliana swelled with pride and couldn't wait to tell Mamma that Byron had done just fine.

"Foster, I just can't understand your animosity toward Wilson and the League," said Grange. "I know you want peace as much as anyone."

"Peace, yes! True peace, though, not a lid over a boiling cauldron. I agree, it sounds perfect—the League of Nations, I mean. Heads of state meeting, agreeing, and working out all their differences over a table, then policing each others' actions. But I just don't believe it will work. Wilson is trying to create a peace that can't be realized until the Lord returns."

"Well, I'm all for it, and I hope Congress approves the United States' joining. We'll soon know, I guess, for they're considering it right now."

Foster scoffed as he laid his napkin down untidily by his plate and turned fully toward Grange, a sharp intensity in his face. "We'll just be jumping into an on-going squabble if we join. It's unrealistic and stupid!"

Byron blinked in surprise, then said hesitantly, "But, sir, don't you think we must make every effort to avoid another war?"

"I think," said Foster, emphasizing his words with sharp stabs of his fork, "I think the disagreements evolving from the League could very well *cause* another war."

All this time Juliana had been trying to finish her mushrooms, and now, having finally swallowed the last slick blob, began to apply herself to a small, dainty dish of peaches and cream. She thought everyone else was absorbed in Wilson and the League and started visibly when Foster exclaimed, "Aunt De! She liked our mushrooms! Here, have some more, Juliana. They're quite good for you. Pinedale grows an abundance of several kinds. These are boleta."

"You mean—" Her hand shook as she laid the serving spoon down. "You picked these—here on your place?"

"Of course. Oh, don't worry," he said with a sudden laugh as he realized her concern. "They're not poisonous. I know how to be sure about that. I break a piece off and, if it turns blue, it's poisonous. Or I test it with my tongue. If it's bitter at all, we know not to use it. This is a very good little mushroom. Since the weather has been warm and rainy, they've popped up all over the woods."

That time she could not eat all the mushrooms, and she felt Aunt De's watchful gaze on her.

"Clean your plate, Juliana!" said Molly in a loud whisper, but as she turned pale at the thought, Miss Sweet said casually, "Oh, don't worry her. I'll add it to Beppo's dish. That dog will eat anything."

Though she was relieved, Juliana felt thoroughly ridiculed for her finicky stomach, and very provoked with Mr. Foster Kirk for the way he kept looking at her even when he was talking to someone else.

After dinner Mr. Kirk showed them his paintings in the studio. Juliana stood perfectly still in front of one, arrested by the mood of the mountain scene. How had he achieved that magnificant blue, the very blue of the mountains? It made her soul throb, which was the only way she knew to describe it to Mamma later. Here was that familiar ache in her when she saw something so beautiful that it seemed she should do something about it.

While the others were discussing the paintings, Juliana looked around the small room. It was orderly, but not immaculate. It seemed natural to find two or three apple cores in the window sill, and bark scattered from an armful of firewood stacked behind the small heater. There was something very comfortable about the overflowing bookshelves and stacks of *National Geographics* on the floor. A blue-and-white porcelain washbowl and pitcher with matching soap dish had been placed on a low marble-topped stand. Again, millions of tiny cracks declared them heirlooms. There was the smell of soap mingled with old ashes, rich pine splinters, and a musty damp cushion smell as if maybe the doors had been left open all night. She glanced into the next room where she could see a desk and the quilted corner of a bed.

"Juliana!" spoke Molly so sharply that she jumped. "Don't stare so. Don't you know it's terribly impolite?"

"I'm—I'm sorry," said Juliana in humiliation. She lowered her eyes and hoped everyone would ignore her, but she felt herself being observed and her cheeks stained hotly crimson.

"She was just interested," said Grange quietly.

"One can show interest without being rude," snapped Molly.

"It really is quite all right," said Mr. Kirk. "I'd like to know what the lady thinks of what she sees."

Juliana was touched by his kindness. He had called her a lady after Molly's humiliating remark. But what *did* she think? What could she say? Everyone was so quiet. Why didn't someone else say something? Then, gratefully, she felt the furry, friendly rub of a kitten at her ankle, and she bent and scooped up a ball of gray that purred against her neck.

"I think your paintings are real," she said, looking at Mr. Kirk confidently. "They're beautiful and they're real, not like pictures at all, more like —poetry."

"Well done, Juliana!" exclaimed Grange, impulsively squeezing her shoulders.

"But how did you ever get that shade of blue?" asked Juliana, emboldened by the kitten's purr and Grange's encouraging hug.

Mr. Kirk looked from her to Grange to Molly, then stepped to his easel and picked up a bit of chalk.

Rubbing it between his thumb and finger, he said, "Just dust really, as all the colors are. Of course I have to mix colors to get the particular effect I'm after. And have you ever noticed how the blue of the mountains is different at different times of the day or year?" He paused as if he expected her to answer, then plunged on. "Somehow one has to be able to see more colors in the subject than usually meets the naked eye. For instance, blues are purplish, pinkish, greenish, cobalt. But I am telling you more than you want to know, I suppose. Here, would you like to feel the medium I use?"

Byron and Juliana each felt the dusty chalk and, at Mr. Kirk's insistence, made small timid strokes on one corner of the sandpaper pinned to the easel.

"Now I'll have your marks in my next picture," said Foster Kirk, and his smile relieved the gauntness of his face and erased momentarily the scowl that lurked around his brow.

"Come now, folks, let's sit on the porch at the cottage," said Miss Sweet. "It's cooler and more comfortable there."

The porch was a wonderful place, shaded by a big persimmon tree whose branches were loaded with ripening fruit. Grange tried his best to get Juliana to try one, but Juliana assured him she knew about persimmons—that she, like a possum, knew when they were best for eating. Mr. Kirk had taken Byron to see his rock collection and returned to the porch just in time to see Juliana playfully hitting Grange with a green persimmon. "I see we've been missing all the fun," he said to Byron.

"You see what you're missing by not having children?" asked Grange, twisting a lock of Juliana's hair around one finger. You really should consider marriage, Foster."

"Yes, indeed, there are any number of ladies desiring to get to know you," said Molly primly.

"None that could put up with his sour ways," declared Miss Sweet, stroking a yellow cat in her lap, the gentleness in her fingers defying the severity of her tight hairdo and her sharp nose.

"That's my loyal aunt for you," said Mr. Kirk with a chuckle, propping one foot up on the stone wall. "Tell me again, Grange, how was it you became such a part of this family—the Hamiltons, is it?"

Grange gave Juliana a gentle shove and sat down beside her in the swing. "I was running away from home and from Georgia Tech," he said, tossing the green persimmon back and forth from hand to hand. "By chance, or by eternal plan, I visited a small Presbyterian church in Cornelia where these wonderful people spied me quickly as a lonesome stranger and took me in. They fed me, worked me, and helped me put the pieces of my life together. Ever since, I have been pestered by this ornery child who, being the youngest of the six, is quite a spoiled brat."

Grange rumpled the back of Juliana's hair as he spoke, causing Juliana to respond with some spirit, even to the point of slapping at his face, but he caught her hand before it made contact and held it tightly.

"I think it's time we started back to meet the train if we don't want to get left," said Molly, frowning at Grange significantly.

"So it is now," said Grange, looking at the angle of the sun as it laid bars across the board floor. He stood and stretched. "Well, it's been wonderful, old chap. You must have dinner with us when you're back in Atlanta. A most delicious meal you prepared, Miss Sweet," he said to that lady who dusted cat hairs from her hands before shaking his own. "It was Yankee cooking at its best," he said gallantly.

"Yankee, indeed! We're as southern as you are, Grange Neal!"

They were starting up the path when Juliana suddenly remembered her hat. "I'll get it for you," said Mr. Kirk and, before Molly had lumbered up the steep terrace, he was back, spinning the hat around on one finger, the blue ribbons shimmering in the sunlight.

"Thank you," said Juliana, smiling up at him, then quickly tying the ribbons under her chin, glad for the shield against the sun—and his searching eyes. Why was it her arms prickled with as much excitement as when she found the first trillium of spring? As she walked on she told herself that when she was alone she would have to try to figure out why it seemed as if she'd seen Mr. Kirk before.

Much later, as Henry drove them home from the train station, clucking affectionately to Maude, Juliana asked curiously, "Grange, how old is Mr. Kirk?"

Grange turned toward her and spoke sharply, all the laughter gone from his eyes. "And why, may I ask, should Foster Kirk's age matter to you?"

CHAPTER 3

CLOVER HILL HAD SOME absolutely magical spots—at least it had always seemed so to Juliana. One she had outgrown now was a tulip tree that leaned far out over Long Bottom Field. Though it shaded the corn, Papa had managed to leave it every year when he cut trees, clearing more new ground. He never really explained why he left it, but secretly they both knew it was so she could continue to climb its smooth gray trunk and perch with her dolls up over the field to watch the men at their work.

Another place she and Byron had always enjoyed was what they playfully called the Potomac River. It was really a bubbling creek that spilled over wide rocks, or around them and under them. There were delightful, splashy little rapids and falls. Often while Papa and Henry were letting their dinner settle, lying back with hats over their faces by the nearby Cold Springs, Juliana and Byron put on their own historical pageants, complete with Mount Vernon, the Capitol, plenty of loud muskets shot by Whigs and Tories, and wonderful victory speeches. That was a place Juliana no longer visited. It would be so lonesome without their childish bang-bangs and shouts of victory, and without the security of Papa's heavy breathing under his hat.

The place called Indian Hill was much nearer the orchard and home. She still liked to walk there when she could slip away from the house. She and Byron had found many a piece of broken pottery there, and it was a good place to look for arrowheads—and wild tiger lilies and wood violets. The woods stopped at the edge of the clover-sweetened pasture on one side, and on another side the hill dropped off steeply toward the little Jenkins Brook where the enchanting Lorna Doone Slide rushed merrily toward Mud Creek and the Chattahoochee River.

Lorna Doone was the heroine in one of Juliana's favorite love stories. She had met her lover at a beautiful falls, a romantic trysting place. The falls at Clover Hill might not be anything like the one in the book, but the children had agreed on the name. With its mossy slide, its boulders to turn the active waters white, and its quiet dark places near the banks—it had to be every bit as beautiful.

And that was, of all favorite places, Juliana's most favorite. She had come here all her life with her problems and her heartaches, as well as to chase crawfish or watch leafboats battle the rapids. There was something about watching the water that calmed her always and helped her sort out her feelings, just as watching a fire in winter might do.

Juliana sat now just below the slide on a grassy bank, dangling her feet in the cool water. She had washed the dishes and then scooted out. It was Sunday, and there would be no more work to do today. Here in the spotty shade, she had dared to remove her hat and fling her hair back over her shoulders. She had taken much ribbing from her family, particularly Byron and Sister, about being so protective of her white skin. But she stubbornly refused to let them change her, and never hoed or went on errands without her hat. Now sweaty ringlets stuck to her face and neck, and she blew a stray wisp out of her eyes.

It had been two weeks since the trip to Foster Kirk's Pinedale, but Juliana had by no means stopped thinking about it. She remembered the friendly little houses in the valley, Miss Sweet and her many cats, and most of all Mr. Foster Kirk. She didn't know why, but she simply couldn't forget him, her mind wheeling back to him like a needle on a compass always pointing north. She had decided she could not have seen him before, yet sometimes his face would swim before her, and the eyes would tease her with a mischievous twinkle. At other times the image in her mind would look so very lonesome with that heavy scowl that she'd wonder again, *Maybe I have seen him somewhere*.

She picked up a mossy oak twig and, breaking it into bits, threw the pieces idly into the stream. At first she wasn't paying any attention to where the bits of stick drifted, but then it became of absorbing interest to see whether they could get past a protruding root in one place, a boulder in another, a fallen limb farther down. She threw a piece into the water, then ran barefoot along the bank, watching its progress. Funny, she thought, how those bits of debris might fight their way miles and miles to the sea. There would be many forces trying to hinder them, but the persistent force of the water moving forward would eventually carry them to the Big Water, unless they washed up somewhere along the creek bank.

She walked back toward the slide, gazing up at the tall trees on Indian Hill, trees that still lived and grew while Papa lay dead in Level Grove Cemetery. Eternity was so impossible to comprehend. She knew what the Bible said, knew Mamma believed it, knew Papa had believed it. But did she? If only she could, then what would it matter what happened, whether the Something she expected—half exultantly, half fearfully—was really good or not? If she could only understand death, she could live without fear.

A breeze lifted her hair and tickled the tiny hairs on her arms. The sound of the wind was whispery and talkative in the trees. She felt an intimacy with the sky, the water, and the trees as she always had, except that now there was a dissatisfaction deep within her, too. Knowing that God was Creator of all and cared about her daily sorrows and happiness had been enough for her until last year. Then she had seen death come to old—and young. Alice Wheeler, flu, age 9; Luke Taylor, flu, age 13; Mike Walker, killed in action, age 19; Andria Adams died giving birth, age 17; Papa died after surgery, age 56. She had mourned the death of these, and she had mourned also the loss of her happy knowledge that one would die only when one was covered with wrinkles as Grandmother had been. Since last year there had been a gnawing inside her to know that God's eternal life was for her, too.

Slowly she put on her shoes, taking meticulous care with the tiny buttons, then tied the ribbons of her hat under her chin.

"I wonder what Mr. Foster Kirk thinks," she said to herself as she walked up the worn wagon road toward the farmhouse. But then, of course, she would never even see him again, much less find out what he thought about eternity.

If she hadn't been in such deep thought, she would have noticed sooner the long brown object lying across one wagon rut. As it was, she saw it just as she was about to place one neat foot right on top of it. She stumbled backwards when she recognized the design of a three-foot copperhead snake. She stood back, her heart racing with the sudden awareness of danger, then laughed shakily. "The poor thing's dead as a doornail," she said with relief.

She studied the coppery-and-beige pattern of interlocking diamonds, leaning forward to touch gingerly the smooth body, then recoiled as it suddenly twitched. The head was quite thoroughly smashed, and there were even wounds along the long body. But it had not been dead long, or it wouldn't be writhing still, and it most certainly had not been in the road when she came down earlier. She stood with hands on hips looking around toward the orchard, the barn, and back toward Indian Hill and its growing shadows. Who had put the dead snake there for her to find? It was an old trick that her brothers and cousins had pulled many times, but she thought by now Byron and

Henry would know she wasn't so easily frightened. Besides, someone had done a very untidy job of killing.

"I could have done better myself," she declared out loud as she stepped over the snake and started to walk on.

But she stopped abruptly when she saw a pair of blue tattered overall legs.

Tilting her head back and back, she looked up into the huge loose-jawed face of Blake Davis. Blake was the middle son of Mrs. Davis, who had the farm next to Clover Hill. Since Mr. Davis had died of flu, it had been harder for Mrs. Davis to keep her retarded son at home. But Juliana was no more afraid of him than she was of snakes—just awed sometimes.

"Blake Davis! You killed this poor snake and tried to scare me with it!" she said, wagging an accusing finger at him, but her lips curled in a smile. "Well, I'll show you how scared I am!"

Turning, she picked up the snake by the tail and started after Blake who paled and stumbled back, holding his hands defensively in front of him. "No, Juliana, no!" he whined.

"All right. But don't you do that anymore, Blake. It's—it's—well, it's just not nice." When his eyes clouded and his head drooped in shame, she said kindly, "Come on to the house and get some teacakes. I'll bet you're hungry."

When she arrived at the house, Blake Davis was plodding along behind her.

"I told you, Mamma," said Henry, leaning his chair back until he was propped against the porch wall. "I told you our Judy would be here soon, bringing something hungry along with her. I just didn't know it would be as big as Blake Davis!"

Juliana slapped Henry's knee affectionately as she went by, pleased at his use of her childhood nickname.

The next day's mail brought a letter for Juliana from Grange Neal. Since he had taken Molly home, it was understandable that Mamma might have a bread-and-butter letter, thanking her for the summer's nursing. Although Juliana had often felt most put upon when she had to walk with slow, lumbering Molly or struggle through a dull game of checkers with her, she knew it was not she who should be receiving this letter. Still, Grange had always written her since she was a little bit of a girl, that is, until he had gotten married. She opened it carefully, as was her custom with any letter, so it would be neat to keep along with her others.

There were two letters in the envelope. She paused in the road, deciding which to read first, and choosing the one that was folded so oddly. It was a short letter, but it took a minute just to get it unfolded. Then it was checkered with creases. A puzzled look turned to pinkness on her cheeks as she read.

Dear Grange,

It was good to have you over at Pinedale the other day. I hope you'll do it again soon. I'll be here for a few months working on some paintings I've been commissioned to do. Aunt De is glad to have me around, I think, though she won't admit it. But Beppo does. By the way, I realized after you left that my dog Beppo had hidden the whole time. He walked with me to meet you, then I didn't see him again until nightfall.

Grange, do you think I might gain the privilege of painting that darned little scrap of nothing you brought with you? Perhaps her brother could come with her? If the portrait is any good, I would give it to her for the experience of painting it. As you know, I've been looking for just such a subject.

See what you can do, and I'll be most grateful.

Yours,
Foster

"A darned little scrap of nothing?" Is that what he thought of her? After calling her a lady and making her feel so important, as if what she thought really mattered, then he had the audacity to call her such a thing!

"Well, he'll wait a hundred years before he gets a portrait of *me!*" she said with a disdainful sniff as she walked quickly along, whipping the letter against her skirt as if to reprimand its author.

Suddenly she remembered there was another letter in Grange's envelope, and she leaned against an oak tree to read it.

Dear Juliana,

You'll soon be back in school and I wish you the very best. Last year was probably the hardest year of your life, my dear, and you need not fear that it will be repeated. You see, I can tell that inside that pretty head of yours there's a lot of puzzling going on. I would help if I could. But I know that you must find the answers to life's questions for yourself.

Please don't let this letter from Foster be a worry to you. I started just to throw it away, but it didn't seem fair to you or to him, so I didn't. It would be a good picture, I'm sure, though he is not a portrait artist. Still, how could it help being good with you as the subject? But beware—if you decide to do it—and be very businesslike and cool with him. Foster Kirk is a good man, but very strange.

If you do decide to have your picture done (and I personally hope you don't), then let me know and I'll set up the time for you. Be sure someone goes with you.

Love,
Grange

He had almost thrown the letter away! Well, it was a good thing he hadn't. She at least deserved the right to say no. And she knew she'd have to say no. Mamma would never allow it. She opened the oddly folded letter again. Grange had said Foster Kirk was a good man, but strange. What was wrong with that? As she remembered Foster Kirk's expressive eyes—lonesome one minute, teasing the next—she could not imagine herself ever being businesslike and cool with him. And how old was the man, anyway? Grange had never said. She thought maybe he was twenty-five, yet she wasn't sure how long it would take an artist to become well known enough to be commissioned to do paintings. He must be quite successful.

When Juliana presented the idea to Henry, he was incensed that Grange would have thought for a minute they would let Juliana pose for an artist.

"He should have sent *me* the letter," he said, slapping the table with his half-read *Constitution*, and causing his fork to rattle on his clean-sopped plate. "I would have known what to do with it. Burn it!"

"Henry! The man only wants to paint her portrait," scolded Sister.

"As successful as he sounds, he can certainly find another model. Didn't Molly say the girls flocked around him?"

"Yes, but there would be none quite like Juliana. Just think of the honor."

"He doesn't have to use Juliana!" he blustered. Then he dropped his voice, "He probably has—other things in mind."

"Like what, Henry?" asked Juliana curiously.

Henry gave her a sour look, then looked significantly at Mamma. "Just—things," he mumbled and, with no further comment, he rose and stomped out of the house, letting the door close loudly just as he seemed to be closing the subject.

Byron looked up from his book. "Mamma, you needn't worry about Mr. Kirk. He's really quite old. I imagine he's at least forty."

"Oh, he couldn't be *that* old!" exclaimed Juliana.

"And besides, that aunt of his—Miss Sweet? She's anything but sweet. Rest assured, even if he wanted to—he couldn't."

"Wanted to *what?*" asked Juliana impatiently.

Byron looked at her, shook his head, and walked out, tucking his book under his arm. Just before he closed the door, he said over his shoulder, "He's a very good artist, Mamma. You'd probably have to pay $100 to get a picture like that any other way."

The teakettle simmered on the back of the stove, sending a drift of steam up against the warming closet where it formed tiny, hot beads. A kitten rolled on the floor, chasing a ball of yarn which had strayed from Mamma's work basket by the hearth. Out on the porch, a metal dipper rattled rhythmically against the wall as the wind stirred by.

"Oh, dear me," said Mamma after studying her broken, stained nails for a long time. "I do wish sometimes that both of you were quite ugly," she said, and then broke into a shaky laugh.

Juliana knew better than to press Mamma to explain what mysterious "things" Foster Kirk could possibly be planning. She would bombard Sister with questions that night after they blew out their light. Sister answered questions better in the dark, she'd found out. And Sister knew quite a bit because she was five years older and had already taught school for a year.

Mamma stood up and pushed her chair snugly against the table. She reached up and repinned a stray lock of hair that had escaped from the bun at the back of her head. Then, as she carefully stacked the plates, she asked, "Do you want to have your portrait done, Juliana?"

Juliana felt a shock of consternation that Mamma would actually ask her opinion on a matter of such importance. "I don't know. I guess so," she answered slowly.

"I'll talk to Henry some more. Maybe he'll change his mind," said Mamma firmly, adding, as if she were not changing the subject, "You clean the kitchen while Sister and I get back out to the washing. We've still got the overalls to scrub."

Henry could not be said to change his mind. He argued stubbornly that the photograph of Juliana which he'd taken to boot camp with him was as pretty a picture as they needed, that Foster Kirk was up to no good, that forty wasn't too old for romantic inclinations. Then with a grunt, he said, "This is just what we could expect from letting Byron and Juliana go off on a Sunday like that."

But after corresponding with Grange and Mr. Kirk, Mamma decided to let Juliana go to Pineland for as many sittings as it took to complete the portrait. Henry would just have to fuss.

The first Saturday Sister went with her, laughingly telling Mamma as they left that if Juliana were put in a trance and placed in an enchanted castle, she would wave her wand and help her escape by a gossamer thread ladder, and would spirit her back home. Juliana was anything but comforted.

CHAPTER 4

THE THREE-MILE BUGGY RIDE to Cornelia, the wait for the train, and the ride on the Tallulah Falls Railway to Hill's Crossing were not long enough for Juliana, who began to panic as the train slowed down to let the girls out. What would she say? How would she sit? How would she introduce Sister properly?

As it turned out, there was a confusing commotion just as they got off the train so that the introduction seemed to take care of itself. A huge black-and-tan German shepherd dog was chasing a pure white, smartly trimmed poodle along the road, down into the brambles, back again, between legs or whatever else impeded the race. Even before the train left with the conductor hanging out the door to watch as long as he could, Juliana could hear a shrill scream above the din of the dogs' barks and Mr. Kirk's thunderous commands to Beppo, the German shepherd.

When the train was gone, a stylish young lady in a

long-waisted lavender dress came dashing across the tracks, her face quite red, her brown ringlets tossing.

"If you have let your dog hurt my Serena, I shall never, never forgive you," she screamed.

At that moment the poodle came out of the bushes, ears flopping, pink tongue hanging, and ran blindly into Juliana's legs. Juliana had been awaiting her chance and now swooped the little dog into her arms, causing Beppo to put on brakes suddenly and bark as he danced around her.

"Beppo!" said Foster once again, and, whether he was more forceful that time, or whether Beppo just finally heard him, the dog did pause in his dancing and barking long enough for Mr. Kirk to get a firm grip on his collar.

"Give me my dog at once!" exclaimed the young woman, and Juliana handed it over, commenting as she did so that, except for a few extra burrs and stick-tights, the little dog was all right.

"And how should you know?" demanded Serena's mistress, hiding her face in the burry fur.

"Let me introduce you to my visitors, Maureen," said Mr. Kirk calmly as if nothing was amiss and they had all just arrived at this lonely country crossing for a friendly chat. "This is Miss Emily Hamilton and Miss Juliana Hamilton from Cornelia." That was when Juliana realized that she needn't worry any more about the introduction. Somehow Mr. Kirk and Sister had gotten themselves introduced.

"And what would you be doing so far from home?" inquired Maureen, stroking her pet and pouting prettily.

"I've come for . . ." began Juliana.

"They've come to see my studio," interrupted Mr. Kirk.

"I thought Miss Sweet said Juliana Hamilton had already been to see your studio. You are Juliana Hamilton, aren't you?"

"Yes, Maureen, she is, but she's brought her sister this time. Now—if you'll excuse us, please."

"Certainly. And I'll also send you the bill if Serena has to have stitches," she retorted. "I do wish you would teach your dog better manners."

"Perhaps if I knew them myself, I could," he said, touching his hat by way of farewell.

Beppo ran back and forth through the woods as they walked to the cottage, his tail wagging as if he'd done a great thing.

"You have quite a fiery dog, haven't you?" asked Sister conversationally.

"It helps to have one that commands respect. I feel safe leaving Aunt De with Beppo to keep watch."

Juliana was wondering how Aunt De could need anyone to keep watch over her, when that lady came walking toward them across the cottage lawn. She was gracious, but cool, her eyes taking in every detail of the girls' attire.

"You must be quite tired," she said to Sister. "Come in, and we'll refresh ourselves before Foster starts the sitting. I do say, Foster, don't you think you've chosen the wrong one for your painting? This one has a much more interesting face."

"Aunt De, will you just serve refreshments and stay out of my art, please."

"Oh, I'll do that. Only while I'm about it, I must say that you're missing something by not doing Maureen Logan's portrait. Now *there's* a face."

"Aunt De!"

"All right, all right! Just never mind an old aunt without a dab of sense."

Juliana drank gratefully from a glass of fresh-squeezed grape juice as she stroked a cat that had jumped into her lap the minute she sat down. "How many cats do you have?" she asked, for today there seemed even more than before. Everywhere she looked she saw the sleek creatures stalking past an open door, stretching and bathing themselves, or staring back at her with golden eyes.

"Right now I have only ten. I gave away most of a litter not long ago. Usually I keep at least a dozen."

"My, and you keep them fed so nicely," observed Sister, setting her glass down and picking up a furry bundle.

"Yes, they like their mice."

"Oh, they're good catchers?"

"Yes, indeed! They catch them and I cut up the mice for them. With my dressmaker shears."

Juliana paled and clapped a hand over her mouth, while Sister stifled a giggle. A solemn Aunt De observed them both with hawk-eyed interest.

"Aunt De, will you cut out your gory stories," remonstrated Mr. Kirk. "Come, Miss Juliana, it's time for us to get to work if we're to get anything done before your train is back."

Sister, being obedient to Mamma and Henry, followed behind Juliana and Mr. Kirk as they walked across to the studio. She entertained herself for some time by looking at all the paintings, but she soon became bored listening to Mr. Kirk tell Juliana over and over to sit up straight, be still, hold her hands thus and so. When she walked back out into the sunshine, she found Aunt De not far away, pulling weeds from around a lilac bush.

"My dear," said Miss Sweet calmly, "perhaps he will do your portrait next. Yours is the face he needs."

"I do most assuredly hope not," said Sister with spirit. "I could never be patient enough."

Juliana's back ached from sitting so straight, her nose itched, and she had a violent urge to cross her legs. Sitting for a traveling photographer, who hid under a black cloth after threatening certain doom on anyone who moved, was nothing compared with this. She was not at all sure she could stand it. Yet she wanted very much to please this tall, stern artist whose rare smiles were well worth the wait. She didn't know why it mattered so much to her, but it did.

"Miss Juliana, you are so stiff and unnatural," said Foster, stepping away from the easel and coming toward her.

"Of course I am. You told me to sit exactly so, and I'm not used to staying still for so long. If you could only let me read a book, maybe . . ."

"A book? You like to read?" The tension in his jaw relaxed. "Let's try that then. *David Copperfield? Swiss Family Robinson? Hound of the Baskervilles? Jane Eyre!* Have you read *Jane Eyre?*" All the time he was pulling books out of the overstuffed case and looking to her for approval. She had been crossing and recrossing her legs in great freedom, but now folded her hands as he turned his full attention toward her.

"I'd like to read that one, please. It was one of my grandmother's favorites, I remember."

As he stood beside her to hand her the book, she was intensely aware of his size, his strength. But when she looked up, what she saw in his face puzzled her—a look of wistfulness? Surely this man could have anything he wanted, couldn't he? She wondered again at his age and was even more determined to find out.

He smiled as he handed her the book. "Do you think now, Miss Hamilton, that you can sit up fairly straight, read without putting your nose in the book—and perhaps be still?"

"I can be as still as one of your waterfalls, sir," she said primly, and he laughed as he returned to his easel.

As she began to read, she wondered why it was that in so little time she felt she knew Mr. Kirk better than her older brothers, Calvin and Richard. Of course *they* treated her like a baby and *he* treated her like a lady—most of the time. That was the difference. But he was every bit as old as they, maybe even older.

On the way home she learned Foster's age. Sister said that Miss Sweet had told her he was two years old when they moved there in 1888, and it didn't take much math to figure out that he was thirty-two or thirty-three now, depending on his birthday. He *was* old then! But he didn't seem old. That wistful look on his lean face came to her hauntingly during the next week as she drew water from the well, picked August apples, or stood patiently being fitted for her new school dress.

CHAPTER 5

WHEN IT CAME TIME for the next sitting, there was no one available to go with Juliana. Byron and Henry were both picking apples and had a crew of paid apple pickers coming to help. Sister needed to do some research in the library in preparation for the new school term. And no one even considered that Mamma might go. Clover Hill simply couldn't operate without Mamma at the hub.

"She'll just have to stay home," said Henry flatly as he pushed away from the breakfast table. "We can hardly spare *her* from the work, much less anyone else. And she doesn't need to go, anyway."

But Mamma was determined to have a portrait of her youngest daughter painted by this artist whom by now she had found featured in back issues of the *Constitution*. He had a serious face and looked as if he would be both honest and thorough. She prided herself on being a good character analyst and felt only the slightest misgivings as she sent Juliana off to Pineland by herself. After all, the man was Grange's friend, and Sister had assured her that Miss Sweet and her cats would be all the chaperones needed.

Foster Kirk paced back and forth waiting for the train, Beppo following his every step. It seemed impossible after all these years that the girl of his dreams had actually materialized. Yet she had come with all the spontaneity, graciousness, natural beauty, and depth of feeling that he could ever have longed for in a companion. The instant his exuberance swelled, the impossibility of any future relationship clamped around him like a vise. For this girl who had appeared to be at least eighteen was, in fact, barely fifteen—just a child. He had not believed Grange at first, felt sure Grange was throwing him off so he could have Juliana for himself, for it seemed quite likely that Molly was not long for this world.

After that first sitting, Foster knew Grange was right. The innocent curve of her cheek, the complete honesty in her eyes, her childish inability to sit still for even five minutes—all confirmed Grange's word, no matter what the motive had been in telling him. Foster's conviction that there would never be a lady in his life as precious as Juliana left him both joyful and despondent. Joyful because, even if he could never have her, it was wonderful to know she actually existed. Painfully, sorrowfully despondent, because he knew there was no way he could ever have her for his wife, and it would be unfair ever to let her know how she affected him.

Beppo growled deep in his throat and Foster sniffed heavy perfume even before Maureen came into view, her dog in her arms. She stopped suddenly and exclained, "Foster Kirk! Don't tell me you're meeting those girls again!"

"You guessed right, Maureen. And how is your summer going?"

"Most fearfully boring, I'm afraid," she said, coming very close, the poodle whining and shaking in her arms as Beppo's ears pricked and his tongue lolled to one side in anticipation of action.

"Boring? In this wonderful country with so many untold mysteries to explore?"

"Now, Foster, don't tell me you don't miss the clamor and excitement of the city. Mother thought I just must spend this summer in the country with Aunt Jill, but I can hardly wait to get back. Won't you be going back soon? I thought you had an exhibit this fall. We shall be sure to be there if you do—Mother and I. She thinks you're just about the best artist this side of Turner."

"Thank your mother for me, will you?" he responded smoothly, sidestepping her question.

One might almost have imagined that he snapped his fingers ever so quietly behind his back. For some reason, anyway, Beppo lost patience suddenly and began barking ferociously around the skirts of Maureen who clutched her pet in panic.

"Better go, I think, before Serena gets hurt," yelled Foster as he grabbed Beppo's collar. He managed to tip his hat politely as Maureen left, a decided pout on her lips.

Maureen was as disgusting to him as all the other painted girls he seemed destined to attract. There was absolutely nothing to her. She would agree to anything that seemed good for the moment. She was undependable, flighty as a feather, and interested only in her silly dog, her shopping sprees and, eventually, in marrying a man with money. But he knew, too, that at twenty-five, Maureen was the "proper" age for him.

His heart beat faster as the train puffed to a stop, and he and Beppo watched the steps expectantly. When he saw her he wondered briefly if one could have a heart attack from beholding too much beauty. There was the slender perfect waist, the sweet rounded figure above it, the intelligent, eager face clothed in a complexion of untouched peaches and cream, the wide blue eyes looking for him, locking with his momentarily, then dropping in that mysteriously lovely way of hers.

When he realized Emily had not come, he went through an inner turmoil, knowing that he had been utterly trusted by the Hamilton family and wondering if he really were trustworthy.

"I'm glad you wore the blue gingham again, Miss Hamilton," he said as they walked along. "It's just the right blue for my picture."

"I didn't know how artists worked," she said, picking an aster as she passed and twirling it like a tiny pinwheel. "I thought it would be frightful if you had gotten to a certain point with blue gingham, then had to switch over to green dotted swiss."

His delighted laugh seemed to fill the woods, ricocheting off the trees. "That would be dreadful."

he said in mock horror. "Actually, though, my memory is pretty good and I'm not *wholly* dependent on what I see at the moment."

"Oh, then you may not really need me any more. Perhaps you have me memorized," she said, a teasing smile playing on her lips as she looked up at him questioningly.

"I'm afraid you don't understand," he said. "The dress is only complementary to the picture and may not in the end be very important. I'm studying your face, and the blue gingham helps to bring out the color of your eyes."

"And you haven't memorized my face? It isn't very big, you know. I've learned poems much longer than my face."

His laughter again burst forth, and Beppo ran back toward them along the path to see what was pleasing his master so much. Foster patted his head and stroked his ears before he answered in a voice first choked with mirth, then growing more and more serious. "A face—like yours—could be studied for a thousand years and never completely memorized, because it changes from moment to moment. I can only hope to capture the moment that seems the most like you."

"That sounds quite difficult to me," she said, contemplating his words with a frown. "Capturing a moment, I mean."

They walked in silence for a ways, going over the top of the hill where Foster had shown them he wanted to build a house, starting down the other side between young hemlocks and tall pines. Juliana gripped a handful of her skirt, then she turned to regard this man whom she had come to respect, wondering whether to open her private world to him. Somehow she felt he might be able to help her as no one else could. Finally she spoke.

"You talked of capturing moments. Do you—what do you think about eternity?"

He looked at her sharply, aware that this was no trivial question. "That's a big one," he admitted softly. "My thoughts on eternity go back to the things my mother taught me. Father was a preacher, but Mother showed me what it meant to love. She died when I was thirteen, and that's when I had to come to grips with what I myself believed."

"That's the way it's been with me," she said, busily pulling pieces of pine bark from a tree where they'd paused. "Papa died last year along with a lot of other people I knew. I've realized I can't go on living on someone else's faith. I need my own."

"But don't get bogged down expecting some fantastic revelation," he said gently. "Just as your face cannot be memorized in a thousand years, God's ways can never be totally understood. I don't accept things very well," he said, his back to her now, flexing a muscle in his jaw, "so I don't feel I have life figured out by any means. But I do feel assured God is in control of eternity—whatever it holds—and, though I may buck and storm, in the end I'm glad He's in charge."

"And you're not afraid to die?"

"Everyone's afraid to die, I guess. No one knows just what it will be like and that scares us. But there's no need to ruin the heaven on this side and the other side of the bridge of death worrying about whether the planks will hold."

"You must be a poet, using figures of speech like that."

"And you must be a good English student to understand figures of speech."

"Who said I understood?" she asked saucily. Then her voice grew more serious as she walked, idly scattering bits of bark along the trail. "I suppose if the planks were to break and the bridge fall down—don't you think God would give us wings then?"

"I do. Whatever death is like, God will be there." He answered so positively, so certainly, that she looked up at him, her face reflecting the relief that flooded her.

"You—you have helped me so much," she said. "Thank you."

"The truth is," he said slowly, watching her profile as he spoke, "that you helped yourself. I was only here. And to me," he added, "knowing how to live this life is much more imminent than what the next one holds."

They said no more as they continued down across the cottage lawn, and soon they were busy in their separate worlds—Foster painting, Juliana reading. Yet there was a togetherness, a peaceful oneness. She felt contented and secure in a way she could not begin to explain. And she was immeasurably grateful that he had not laughed at her concerns, but had taken them to heart as if they were his own.

She stole a glance at his face, visible above the back of the easel. His heavy brows were furrowed in deep concentration, his mouth set in a firm line. *Even when he is grim, he is so very handsome,* she thought and then wondered why he'd never married. Perhaps someone had broken his heart and that was why his eyes harbored such sadness at times.

She dropped her eyelids quickly as he looked up, and spoke sharply, "Be still, Juliana!" She could not know that the roughness of his manner concealed the overwhelming tenderness he felt for her at that moment.

CHAPTER 6

JULIANA LOOKED FORWARD each week to reading the next installment of *Jane Eyre*. Jane was the orphan girl who served as governess to a small child in a mysterious old house and fell in love with the child's father, a widower twice Jane's age. Juliana was so completely absorbed in the bitter-sweet story that she sometimes forgot and swung her foot back and forth or rested her chin on a curved forefinger, but a peremptory throat-clearing by the artist would remind her of her pose.

Always she dreaded seeing Miss Delia. That lady seemed to bore holes right through her, which let her self-confidence run out until she felt flat and plain. Several times Maureen Logan was there visiting Miss Sweet, and then it was even worse. Juliana had the distinct feeling that she was being compared to the elegant Miss Logan and was coming out on the short end every time. Secretly she wished Mr. Kirk would just do Maureen's face and forget about hers, but she dared not bring up the subject. Part of her rebelled at the thought of the triumph in Maureen's eyes should Mr. Kirk decide to follow her suggestion. She honestly didn't think Mr. Kirk would mind too much one way or the other. Didn't he just want the experience of painting a portrait? But then he could have asked Maureen to start with if he had wanted to.

Ever since Juliana had learned Mr. Kirk's age, she'd tried to think of him only as a big brother or an older friend like Grange, but none of the roles had fit him just right. The man was disturbing—a person who could not and would not be ignored. He seemed to want her to understand him, yet he was so different from anyone she'd ever met. And, she decided, he actually *enjoyed* being odd. For instance, he declared once while pounding one fist into the other palm, that he would take anyone to court who was caught hunting on his well-posted land. "Hunting, as a sport, is abominable," he said with dark eyes flashing. She wondered what he would think of her brothers' occasional coon and 'possum hunts, but never got up the courage to ask.

Since their talk about eternity, they had had many more conversations along the wooded pathway from Hill's Crossing, had looked together at the tiny eggs in a vireo's nest, had discussed the differences in pine trees so that now she recognized white pines, red pines, jack pines, and tall, straight short-leafed yellow pines. He showed her a bed of maidenhair fern, ferns that grew out from a center like a head of hair, and he let her smell the broken pieces of a sweet fern.

They were standing on Hilltop, looking at the distant blue dips of Trey Mountain. He had explained to her that there were actually three peaks on the mountain, thus the name 'Trey,' but that from this side only two could be seen.

"You love your place, don't you, Mr. Kirk?" she asked.

"It has always been my dream to enlarge it and make it a sanctuary for wild animals. And . . ." He paused, thrust his hands in his pockets, and studied the mountain peaks.

"And what?" she prompted.

"I want to raise a family here . . . have children to roam the woods."

"That would be wonderful!" she exclaimed. "You will do it, Mr. Kirk! I know you will!" she said, touching his sleeve impulsively.

He turned toward her and she wanted to cry out at the look of pain in his eyes.

"Is something—wrong?" she stammered.

"Yes, but nothing you can help," he replied in such a clipped way that she kept silent as they walked on.

Juliana was to see the hurt in his face once again that same day. He had painted for some time while she read. Sensing a change, she looked up from her book to see Mr. Kirk standing back, head cocked, hands on hips, studying first the picture, then her.

"When are you going to let me see, Mr. Kirk?" she asked brightly, closing her book.

"Not before you stop calling me Mr. Kirk and use my given name instead. I'm really quite tired of formality."

She blushed peony-red and dropped her eyes until all he could see was the top of her blond head. "But, M—Mr. Kirk," she stammered, "It would be unmannerly for me to call you by your first name. After all, we—that is, I . . . the difference in our ages, you know," she finished miserably.

"What about Grange?" he asked in a tight voice. "He's almost as old as I am, and you call him by his first name."

She looked up in confusion. "But Grange is different . . ." she tried to explain, but paused when she saw the wistful sadness fall across his face like a curtain.

"I see. Sorry," he said.

Even Miss Sweet chided him for being rude that day as he rushed Juliana up the path. "Don't hurry the child so," she called out. "Her legs aren't half as long as yours."

Foster Kirk barely spoke as they waited for the train. Then he said with an attempt at cheerfulness, "I'll let you see the portrait next week. It will be your last sitting."

She should be glad that there was only one more sitting, she thought as she rode home. It had not been easy sitting so still for an hour, and she knew she needed to help at Clover Hill. Henry had not been gracious, but at least he had allowed the sittings, and now it would be over. Life could go back to normal. She would have more time for her homework, too. Now that October was here the teachers seemed to take joy in loading her with assignments, and she liked to do everything with meticulous thoroughness. Now she would not be disturbed any more by visions of Foster Kirk.

But she felt strangely dismal at the thought rather than relieved. Shifting in her seat she stared out at the passing scenery, trying to rid herself of an aching emptiness she could not explain.

That night as she tried to sleep, Juliana's mind turned again to Foster Kirk. She knew she could never forget the things he had taught her about God and life and beauty. She smiled to herself in the moonlit room as she considered how she would describe Mr. Kirk to her children one day: "He was a tall man—dark, stern, friendly and laughing one minute—sad the next." He would be quite famous by then, and she would tell them how once he had talked to her as if she were very important, and had held her hand helping her down from the train. Picturing him with his dog there at the crossing, she was suddenly stabbed by the memory of pain in his eyes.

He wanted her to call him Foster. Why should it matter so much? For some reason, though, it did. She reached out and traced a moonlit shape of window-pane, distorted by the heavy folds of the quilt. Why would it be disrespectful if she called him by his first name? It would be their last time together. And, if it would bring the sunshine to his eyes, it would be well worth the effort. Having reached a decision, she dropped quickly off to sleep.

She practiced saying his name the day before the sitting as she sat by the talking waters of Lorna Doone Slide. As she practiced over and over, it began to sound more and more natural. "Hello, Foster." "Did you have a good week, Foster?"

"Juliana, what on earth are you doing?" asked Byron, flopping down beside her.

"How dare you creep up on me like that?" she snapped.

"But I didn't. I just walked up and you were talking away, so you didn't hear me. What were you talking about, anyway?"

She heaved an inner sigh of relief. "Just silly stuff," she said. "You wouldn't be interested." She quickly changed the subject. "Remember how we used to catch spring lizards and make pots from the brook clay?"

"Not in cold October water, though. And back then you would have told me if you were mooning about somebody." He would not be diverted. "It's Foster Kirk, isn't it?"

"Byron! I was not mooning."

"What, then?"

"None of your business."

"I think it is. You're my sister, a rascally one, but pretty precious all the same. I don't want you to be hurt."

"And I won't be," she said stoutly.

"When will the picture be finished?"

"Tomorrow."

"Good, then maybe we can get back to normal around here. I've been missing you."

"Missing me! How could you miss anyone, as wrapped up in your books as you are? You even take a book to milk the cows!"

"Thought maybe the cows could do with a little education," he said with a grin.

Juliana intended to greet Foster by name as soon as she arrived, but it didn't work that way. He was very abrupt and businesslike, and talked more to Beppo on their walk than to her. As a matter of fact, she had to take several quick, running steps to catch up to his determined stride.

She read quickly that day, trying to finish *Jane Eyre* before she had to leave for the last time. Everything was still except for the purring of two or three cats, and the chattering of birds outside. When Mr. Kirk groaned, Juliana jumped visibly, then rose from her chair with a gasp as he snatched the painting off the easel and threw it down on the window seat.

"What's wrong?" she asked, marking her place in the book with her finger.

"Everything!" he said in utter exasperation. "I can't get the feeling . . . the mobility . . . even the color is wrong."

"But I've been still, Really, I have! Was I that bad a subject?"

"No, no! It's not you. It's my own lack of ability to capture—your pensiveness and expectancy."

"Mr. Kirk, it's only a picture. Please don't be upset," she said, laying the book down and stepping toward him.

"Only a picture?" he echoed, looking out the window. "No picture in which an artist invests himself is 'only' a picture . . . this one in particular."

Juliana felt rebuked. She knew nothing about art except what he had taught her, but did he have to make her feel so ignorant? What did he mean by "This one in particular"? Could it be because he had not painted a portrait before? That must be it. This was his first.

"You will do better with the next one," she soothed.

"The next one?"

"Yes. Why don't you ask Maureen to sit for you next? With her dog? Maureen's hair has much more color than mine." Her voice raced to keep pace with her growing idea. "And she would be quite pretty if you would let her smile for you."

She could not understand his total silence. She knew only that he was very upset, judging from the muscles in his neck that were working like ropes, and his hands, fisted hard in his pockets. Quietly she slipped up behind him and looked around the bulk of him at the painting which lay face up on the window seat. She was shocked when she saw it. Though a pretty picture, the woman in it didn't look anything like her. Why, after all that talk about getting the color of her eyes right, had he painted her profile with her eyelids almost closed, as if she were sleepy? No wonder he was upset! It really was not a good likeness at all. But she must think of some way to console him.

Shyly she touched his arm and said softly, "I think it's quite good—Foster."

She never knew how it happened, but the next moment his arms were around her, one big hand crushing her head against his chest. He held her that way for a time, and she wasn't sure whether it was her heart or his beating so loudly—only that she wanted to stay there forever with his cheek against her hair.

"Juliana?" he whispered, turning her face up to his.

She saw warmth and joy in his eyes, felt the tenderness of his hands cupping her face. The ecstasy tingling through her whole body made her aware of life in a way she had never experienced before. Was this the Something Big she had known was going to happen? She felt delightfully secure in the strength of Foster's embrace. But an alarm went off in her head just as he leaned toward her, his mouth just inches from hers. She began to push with both hands against his chest, and he let go so suddenly he had to catch her hand to keep her from falling. He dropped it quickly and turned back toward the window.

"I'm sorry, Juliana—" His voice was strangely choked. "Will you forgive me?"

"Yes, of course I'll forgive you. But you mustn't do that ever again," she warned, frowning darkly. Her brother Henry would have been proud of her, for she sounded quite severe and very grown-up. "And now I must be going. Shall I take the painting with me?"

"No! That is—I wanted to put it in a frame and I thought perhaps I could bring it to you. Next Saturday?" She would not look into his eyes, though she felt them demanding her attention.

"I don't know," she faltered. "My brothers will not like it, particularly Henry."

"Juliana, what I did was very wrong, but you said you forgave me. Only a few minutes ago—wouldn't you have agreed to let me come?"

She considered the truth of his implication, and nodded slightly.

"Well, then, if you truly forgave me, we can start over. . . . We can be friends again, can't we?"

After a long moment, she changed the subject in tacit acknowledgment of his plea. "Are you sure you know how to find Clover Hill?"

"Yes, certainly. Grange has told me so much about it. Come now, we must go and meet your train. Here—take the book. I know you didn't finish it. I'll pick it up next week."

If Miss Sweet noticed that Juliana's hair was slightly mussed and her color high, she didn't mention it. But as the two started up the hill, she called out to Foster to stop by Maureen's house before he came back and get a recipe she'd been promised. "Don't forget now!" she called peremptorily, and Juliana looked back to see her standing, arms folded across her breast, her long skirt rippling with the insistent circling of a cat. A hot prickling of rebellion added itself to the confusion in Juliana's mind. What right had Miss Sweet to decide to whom her nephew should pay his attentions?

CHAPTER 7

JULIANA DID NOT TELL anyone, even Sister, what had happened to her. But she had to explain why she still did not have the painting.

"That man is trying to poison our family!" exclaimed Henry when he heard Foster was coming. "He will bring nothing but trouble."

"Henry, that's not fair," said Mamma, smoothing a quilt square in her ample lap. "You've never met the man, and neither have I. I think it's time we did."

"I tell you he's after Juliana—and the only way he's going to get her is over my dead body!"

Juliana sat quietly in a corner, her hair curtaining her face, the light from the fire glinting on her needles as she knitted a cap for Calvin's little boy, Peter. She wished desperately that she had never left Clover Hill that Sunday morning. Yet at the same time she could not imagine not knowing Foster Kirk. Why, he had become part of the fiber of her thinking. He had helped her to see, and hear, and feel everything more clearly, to be sharply aware of shadow effects, leaf markings, bird calls. Yes, and he had helped her to face the future confidently. Now, though, she wondered if he would be anywhere at all in that future.

She simply could not forget his taking her in his arms, his hand on her head holding her hard against him. And if she couldn't forget, then she knew she couldn't be to him just what she'd been before that episode in the studio. Neither of them could ever be quite the same again. She blushed in the firelight as she wondered what it would have been like if he had really kissed her. She had finished reading *Jane Eyre*, and she reckoned that Foster Kirk was much younger than the hero in the story. But it was only in a book, she reminded herself, that a girl could be happily married to a man twice her age.

"Juliana, I wonder that you can see one stitch in that dark corner," said Mamma, breaking into her thoughts. "Come over here by the lamp light." As Juliana pulled her chair closer, Mamma admired the neat, even stitches she was making. "You've really improved on your knitting, haven't you? Remember how you begged to make sweaters for the soldiers during the war?"

"Yes," she laughed, struggling to emerge from her daydream, "And you would only let me knit cotton washcloths—square, thick things. I wonder if the soldiers ever really used them."

Mamma smiled at her from across the table. "Of course they did."

"But I never got any notes the way you did."

"Wasn't that exciting, Mamma?" interjected Sister. "Getting thank-you notes from the boys who wore your sweaters? The Red Cross did a wonderful thing involving American women in helping to keep the Allied army warm."

"It was a good thing," agreed Mamma. "The poor boys had few enough comforts during that awful time."

"Now you're about to get morbid," said Henry gruffly, adjusting a log in the fire and letting the poker clang back against its corner resting place. He straightened, stretched, then started toward the door. "I'll go see if Maude and the other horses are all right before I turn in," he said.

"Henry and his horses!" said Sister with a little laugh, closing up the book she'd been studying. "I'll bet he wouldn't be so huffy if it were feedbags we'd been knitting!"

Everyone seemed surprised when Calvin, Winnie, and the children rattled up to the door after dark on Friday night. Then, as Juliana was unbuttoning little Peter's coat, she overheard Henry say to Calvin in a low voice, "Glad you could make it, old boy. Just felt we all needed to be here."

"What about Richard?"

"He couldn't be away from the bank tomorrow. Anyway, he's too hot-tempered. It's better this way."

Juliana could barely remember Brother's graduating from high school. In her memory he had always been a man, a stern extra father who seemed able to read her inmost thoughts. Henry talked hard and was very sparing with his affection, but she knew Henry really cared. Somehow she had never been sure about Brother.

Rebellion festered inside her now. So they expected trouble, did they? It was all Juliana could do to act for the rest of the evening like the same carefree girl of a week ago, to be caught up in playing jacks with Margo or taking Peter on piggy-back rides. How she wished she could be that child again, but a door had been opened, and she had walked into a wider place with more possibilities for hurt and happiness. And part of the hurt was in not being trusted. What did they think she would do?

On Saturday morning there was so much activity that Juliana scarcely had time to remember that this was the day Foster Kirk was coming. There were chickens to be caught for Mamma to kill and dress for Sunday dinner, turnip greens to be picked and washed tediously leaf by leaf, scrubbing, dusting, shining, and all the time the babies wanting her to play with them. They, like everyone else, apparently considered her still a child.

When she dusted her borrowed copy of *Jane Eyre* in the room she shared with Sister, she suddenly recalled the significance of the day. She took pains to brush her hair some extra strokes, take off her apron, and volunteer to do the mending so she could keep vigil on the front porch.

By midafternoon Juliana had grown weary of sewing on buttons, patching tears, and sewing up rips, and Margo was begging her to climb a tree with her when the distant throb of a machine caught their attention. Since very few autos passed Clover Hill, she was tempted to grab Margo's hand and run to see. She was glad she hadn't as the roar came closer and closer and she realized the vehicle was not just passing by. She barely had time to stack her work neatly and smooth the wrinkles in her dress when the car stopped in front of the house and Mr. Kirk unfolded himself from it. He took the steps in two strides, then stood in front of her, hat in hand.

"How do you do?" she said politely. "I didn't know you had a car."

"I borrowed it from a friend. . . . You have company," he said, kneeling to meet Margo face-to-face.

"I'm not company," said Margo stoutly. "*You* are."

"This is my brother's little girl," explained Juliana.

"And we live in Nacoochee," said Margo who was anything but shy. "We came all the way down here yesterday, because Daddy said . . ."

Juliana put a hand over Margo's mouth just as Mamma and Sister, hearing their voices, came out on the porch. Mamma looked at Juliana, expecting a proper introduction. But Juliana became suddenly tongue-tied, so Sister did the honors. Mamma invited Foster into the front room.

The front room was both living room and bedroom. Mamma kept her prettiest spread on that bed. It was one she had crocheted with fine white thread in a delicate flower pattern. At the windows were thin white curtains, pulled back with tatted ties. Over the narrow mantle hung a photograph of the whole Hamilton family, including Grandmother and Papa, and around the room were other pictures: a framed *Saturday Eve-*

ning Post cover, a print of a broken farm wagon with a hatless farmer trying to take a wheel off.

The freshly-lit fire cast flickering reflections in the polished floor, the shiny Edison phonograph, and the backs of Grandmother's Duncan Phyfe chairs. The fire was mainly for looks as it wasn't really cold, but Juliana was grateful for its added cheer. Though the room was filled with happy memories of Christmasses past, more recently it had held the strange chill of an open coffin with Papa's profile in the shadows. She wished they could have sat today in the dining room around the big table, the everyday warm family gathering place. But Mamma wouldn't have thought it a proper place to receive a first-time guest.

Juliana was fascinated by the easy flow of conversation between Mamma, Mr. Kirk, and Sister. They were talking about some of the new electrical gadgets on the market. Mr. Kirk had seen a vacuum cleaner demonstrated in a store in Atlanta and was impressed with its capabilities.

"I don't think you'd have much need of it here," he said, glancing around the neat, shining room, "but some folks would find it quite handy. The nice thing about it is it doesn't stir up the dust."

"You've convinced me, Mr. Kirk," said Mamma, with an unaccustomed twinkle in her eye, "that if I ever have electricity, I'll want a vacuum cleaner the very first thing—well, the first thing after an iron. How marvelous—not to have to heat and reheat those heavy irons, but to have one evenly heated, light instrument. I don't suppose you have seen one of those at work?"

"Actually, my landlady in Atlanta uses one." He chuckled and leaned forward. "She confided in me that she thought ironing would be like play with her new iron, but she had to admit it was still hard work."

"It's unbelievable, isn't it, that this time last year one could hardly buy the bare necessities, and now folks are getting all those luxuries," said Sister.

"Yes, but I'm afraid it won't last." Mr. Kirk was suddenly serious. "After this rush there is likely to be a depression."

"You really think so?" asked Mamma anxiously. "Henry said the same thing. By the way, where is Henry? I thought they were coming. Juliana, run fetch your brothers, please, and when you come back, you may bring the refreshments out from the kitchen."

Juliana left obediently, but her pride was damaged. What was Mr. Kirk to think—that she was a servant or something? But what did it matter what he thought? She had to take herself to task over her own inconsistency. One minute she wanted to be far away from the sound of Foster's deep resonant voice; the next, she was fuming for being banished from his presence.

The refreshments were not served after all. Juliana met her brothers coming in and, as they washed up, she began to prepare a tray. "Don't bother with that," said Brother, drying his hands.

"But Mamma said . . ."

"Never mind. We won't need it."

Winnie came in from her walk with Margo in time to hear Brother's curt remark.

"Do you really think you must?" she asked quietly at his elbow.

"Yes. There's no doubt it must be done."

"Well, do be quiet about it and don't wake Peter from his nap."

Byron shifted his feet in obvious misery and hung behind the other two as they literally stomped into the front room. Juliana thought she would never ever forget the rude way Brother demanded to see the portrait, how he made it clear there were to be no more calls, and how Henry offered to pay for the portrait that they not be beholden to Mr. Kirk. She stayed outside the door, ashamed to be in the same room with them. She heard Mamma murmuring something about how beautiful the picture was, and Henry saying, "But, you see, Mamma. He's painted her as a woman instead of our little girl."

She couldn't see Mr. Kirk, but she could imagine his dark expression, heavy brows drawn together, as he said, "There will soon come a time, gentlemen, when you will have to recognize that your sister is no longer a child."

Juliana heard a quick movement and then the squeak of the door leading onto the porch. "Please leave, sir," said Brother icily, "and I suggest that you never darken these doors again. We may be simple country folk, but we're not dumb to the wiles of the world, and we will not be taken in."

Juliana shrank farther into the shadows as she heard Mr. Kirk's footsteps on the porch. There was a bewildering silence, and she wondered if he would just leave without saying anything more. She couldn't blame him if he never wanted to think of the Hamilton family again after being treated so for making a friendly visit. Or was it just a friendly visit? His next words, spoken with steely determination, caused her to tremble.

"You have something against artists, I perceive. I came here intending to be open and honest, and I will leave the same way. Rest assured, Mr. Hamilton, you have not heard the last from me."

During the next two weeks, Juliana was aware of Foster Kirk's various attempts to persuade the Hamiltons that he would only visit as a friend until she was older and could make her own decisions. He wrote letters which were masterpieces of reasoning. He made every excuse for dropping by: buying apples, coming to collect the book he'd loaned Juliana, making sketches of Clover Hill House, but time after time he was told to leave, and never allowed even a glimpse of Juliana. Mamma might have weakened and invited him in, but she didn't dare make matters worse than they already were.

Foster startled her one day by walking up into the yard, whistling, no horse or auto anywhere in sight.

"You surely did not walk from Clarkesville?" she asked, astonished to see him on foot.

"Certainly. It's only ten or eleven miles. Just enough to get one well warmed up."

"Look, Mr. Kirk, I believe you're an honest man and I respect you. But you're being most unfair to all of us, particularly Juliana. It's quite obvious to me that, whether you will admit it or not, you are . . ."

"In love with your daughter," he finished for her,

leaning back against a porch pillar since she has not invited him to sit.

She looked at him, wide-eyed. "Then you do admit it. Mr. Kirk, don't you realize how impossible it is? Why, Juliana's room is still lined with dolls she hasn't had the heart to give away. In school she has normal friendly relationships with the other children—including boyfriends who do such mischievous things as dip locks of her hair in their inkwells or drop spiders down her neck. Leave her alone, please, and let her grow."

"That's exactly what I intend to do. Only I want to continue to be her friend and when the time comes. . ."

"Mr. Kirk, you don't understand! The time will never come when she is the right age for you. Can't you accept that? Go look for a lady in Atlanta, a mature lady suitable for an artist of your renown. And—please—leave our Juliana alone!" There were tears in Mrs. Hamilton's voice, and Foster Kirk turned away from her, gripping the squared edge of the porch pillar.

"I agree with you. It *is* impossible," he said at last. "But there is a thing called hope, too, and I cannot give up. All these lonely years I've known that, however tempting it might have been to choose a companion because she was attractive and available, I must wait for the one who would really be a mate in the truest sense—a companion of the mind and soul. As impossible as it must seem to you who are her mother, Juliana *is* that companion, and I will wait as long as I must. If I am not to see her in the meantime, then you must tell me when I may see her again.''

Mrs. Hamilton sat down hard in a wicker rocker, and the fast rhythmic squeaks of the chair spoke of her agitation.

''When Juliana is eighteen, you may come to call on her again,'' she said heavily.

A cool wind rattled the metal dipper that hung near the well. A chicken cackled, proclaiming a fresh egg. Mr. Kirk turned slowly to look into Mrs. Hamilton's face, then put his hat on, and walked away without another word. She watched him disappear along the wooded road and still sat, a corner of her apron twisted hard around one finger.

''But I don't want to leave Clover Hill,'' said Juliana tearfully. ''You said he would not be back.''

''Yes. But the hope he spoke of—it's very strong. I just want to be sure. Your brother will be kind to you, Juliana. He loves you and wants only the best for you.''

''I imagine he'll be the best teacher you'll ever have,'' said Byron, trying to be encouraging.

''But I'll be so far from home.''

''It will only be for the rest of the school year. Nacoochee is a beautiful valley. We lived there once when you were just a baby, before we moved back here to take over the farm. You'll love the place.''

''May I please wait until after Thanksgiving?'' asked Juliana, her eyes like dark pools.

Mamma bit her lip, walked to the window and looked out at the gray sky, then turned. ''No, you must go on Saturday. Brother will come to get you. It's the only way,'' she said, and Juliana knew it would be useless to argue.

CHAPTER 8

NACOOCHEE WAS TWENTY MILES away, a hard half-day's journey by surrey. It might just as well have been a hundred as far as Juliana was concerned, for she could not go home at all for weeks, and at Christmas only for a short holiday.

She longed to hear warm sprays of milk hissing into a metal bucket, and to smell the cows eating their hay. She wanted to see the icicles formed around the edges of Lorna Doone Slide, to scatter cracked corn for the chickens in the evenings, to see the sun set behind the oaks over toward the Davises, and to ride to school with a hot apple tart warming her mittened hands. She wanted to see Henry's new dog Spring, a collie cross who just showed up there one day and refused to leave. Henry had written her about Spring and how she followed him everywhere he went. She didn't know that Henry had sat for hours with his farm record books open in front of him, wondering how he could tell her that he missed her intensely.

Brother's position as Latin teacher at Nacoochee School brought him a very small salary, but his house, a two-story hard by the school campus was provided. He also was pastor of a tiny church. One could see the quaint steeple and hear the bell ring from far up the hillside on Brother's front porch. The hill rose steeply, thickly wooded above Brother's house, and across the valley one could see the sister ridge with spruce and pine spearing the sky. Far beyond, sometimes draped in clouds, was Yonah Mountain.

It was a beautiful valley, as Mamma had said, with rich pastureland surrounding an old sacred Indian mound with a tiny gazebo on its flat top. Juliana, always interested in history, in how other people had lived and died, now showed no interest in the Indian mound or in anything else. But she went dutifully to class, did what she was told to do around the house, and entertained Margo for hours on end, playing dolls with her, having tea parties, sewing up tiny bonnets and aprons. Winnie told Brother one day that Juliana seemed every bit as much of a child as Margo, and she herself could not see what all the problem was about. That a grown man like Mr. Kirk could want a little slip of a girl for a bride was simply unthinkable.

"You heard him yourself, Winnie," Brother reminded her. "But here lately I've noticed Juliana withdrawing more and more. I'm afraid she'll never be the same again. I wish she'd never met that man!"

Juliana heard the exchange between Brother and Winnie as she came down the stairs. She wanted to scream that it wasn't Foster Kirk who was making her withdraw; it was being so far from Clover Hill. If only they would let her go home! As she gripped the smooth stair rail and bit thoughtfully on her lower lip, she suddenly realized that perhaps if she could show them she was quite happy, they would consider her cured and let her go. Surely by now Mr. Foster Kirk had forgotten all about her and would not bother them any more.

She began to will herself to take notice of things around her—the fields of winter beige meeting spruce-clothed slopes that yielded to a blue sky, the roar of the Chattahoochee River in the near distance, and the mysterious Indian mound. All this time she'd been going to school, she had scarcely noticed the people around her. Now she realized that the inevitable cliques had formed and left no room for her, for when she spoke to the girls in the hallway between classes, they looked startled, answered politely, and then turned away. She never had been without a friend before. Her heart became heavier still. Yet she had made up her mind to be happy, so she plunged more deeply into her studies, finding there a challenge that excited her.

She asked to go for a walk one brittle blue afternoon when the wind was moaning like ghost cries in the trees. For once Winnie refused to let Margo walk with her, whether because of the cold wind, or because of a rare perception of Juliana's need for some time to herself. She hushed the child's cries with a teacake, and said to Juliana, "Wrap up good or you'll be sick, and be a dear and pick up some flour at the mill—just half a peck."

It was a long walk and Juliana was grateful for it. She missed so much her solitary tramps in the woods, not just for the chance to find interesting things, but to be alone, to think and consider. Margo was her one bright joy, for she felt needed and loved by her, but today it was good to be alone.

This path to the mill took her up a long straight stretch of road to the river, then along the river a ways and across it. She paused on the bridge and looked down at the water flowing forever and forever on. Something caught in her chest. It was that feeling again such as she had not felt in a long time—that feeling of Something Big about to happen. The water gave it to her—the water rushing along, eager to get wherever it was going, just following the path laid out for it, never knowing what was around the bend. Somehow it reminded her of Foster and his paintings.

She had asked him one day why it was that every painting gave her the feeling of needing to turn the page to see what was next, even though there was no page to turn. His face had lit up with pleasure, and he had explained enthusiastically how that was his very intention. "By using bends in trails, streams, roads, I like to lead a person to wonder what is beyond. Because, you see, there is always a beyond."

Always a beyond, she thought as she watched the water. Always a challenge ahead—mountains, valleys, steep winding trails, tough tests. And always God, too, around every bend. Always He was there. She shook herself and pulled her coat closely around her, noticing for the first time a swinging footbridge not far down the river. Why had she never seen it before? Obviously, it was well used, for the trail leading to it was quite beaten. As she hurried on toward the mill, she promised herself that when she came back she'd cross the footbridge.

Not far up the other side of the river was the mill —waterwheel splashing, rugged gray boards dark under a huge, protective spruce. Juliana stopped again and sucked in her breath at the beauty of the falls, the mill, the waterwheel, the spruce. Since Winnie had very little storage space and bought her flour and meal in small amounts, Juliana had seen these familiar sights often. But today seemed like the first time, as if she'd finally awakened from a restless sleep.

Inside the mill Juliana studied the intricate entanglements of dust webs in the corners of the room while the miller was filling her bag. She sniffed appreciatively at the dusty grain smell that reminded her so much of corn-shucking days at Clover Hill. And she wrote her name in the flour dust of a rough board table.

"Want that I put yer bag in a paper, Miss, so's not to spile yer nice dress?" yelled the miller over the roar of the river and flipping rhythm of the waterwheel.

"Yes, thanks," she nodded and felt a wave of warm gratitude for the little gray-headed man whose eyes seemed pale and washed-out from looking at so much flour.

She walked around the foot of the mill before lifting her eyes to the powerful waterfall crashing from its battlements, stamping its feet into the unyielding rocks below. Holding the flour under one arm, she started back to Brother's. She'd forgotten her mittens, but coming over with only an empty sack to tuck under her arm, it had been a simple thing to keep her hands snug in her coat pockets. Now one hand or the other had to haul the flour. She changed hands frequently, but still each one in turn ached, then numbed in the cold.

As she approached the swinging bridge, she walked slower and slower. Could she walk it? Did she dare? Many others before her had managed it. Yet the bridge was long, and there was only a rope on one side to hold to. She looked both ways to see if anyone were in sight. Seeing no one, she stepped onto the planking and giggled softly as she walked, balancing herself with the sack of flour. It was the next best thing to walking on air. The trick, she realized, was to step lightly and rhythmically so as not to bounce herself off into the water.

She stopped in the middle to watch the water tumbling underneath, splashing wildly white around the rocks, flecks of foam riding out to the banks. There, where the water pooled in places behind boulders, she could see the dark shapes of fish darting around. "'Out of the hills of Habersham, down the valleys of Hall, I hurry amain to reach the plain, run the rapid and leap the fall,'" she quoted happily, knowing that Sidney Lanier must have felt such joy.

She had not worried that anyone would hear her because the wonderful chuckling of the river would cover her voice. But it also covered the sound of approaching footsteps, so that she was completely unprepared for the sudden swinging of the bridge. She had just leaned over slightly to watch the water flow under the bridge and now gave a startled cry. In gaining her balance by grabbing the hand rope, the sack of flour slid out of the miller's protective paper and landed with a plop in the stream.

"Sorry to startle you!" shouted a boy with an amazing profusion of black hair, and with blue eyes that said quite plainly he wasn't sorry at all—had, in fact, *intended* to startle her.

"How dare you, Jason?" she demanded. "Look what you've done! Winnie will think I've been terribly careless."

"Well? You were. Don't you know better than to lean over a swinging bridge? You could have fallen in yourself."

"And if I had?"

"I would have rescued you, of course, and then you couldn't go on ignoring me the way you have. Here, come on off this thing before we both fall." He tried to take her hand, but she stuck one in a pocket and held firmly to the rope with the other.

"I haven't been ignoring you," she said as they stopped on firm land.

"Me and everyone else, too. What are you—stuck-up or something? Just because your brother's a teacher doesn't give you the right to act so high and mighty."

She gulped in dismay. Had she seemed so? No one ever before had accused her of being stuck-up.

"I'm sorry, Jason. It's just that I've been so homesick."

"Well, everyone goes through that. But at least you're with your brother. Some of us don't see our families all year. So come on now and we'll get you some more flour. I have a quarter just burning a hole in my pocket."

"Oh, but you mustn't do that. I'll explain to Winnie. I'm not afraid of her."

"Who said you were? It's my fault, and I don't mind at all shouldering the blame. Actually, it was worth it every bit to see the sparks fly from your eyes. I always knew you'd be beautiful if someone could just make you mad."

She laughed out loud at his boldness and was surprised at a surge of happiness inside. Hadn't she just a short while ago felt as if Something was about to happen? Maybe Jason was at least part of it. She hoped he would be her friend.

She learned on the walk back home that, like her, Jason was interested in Indian lore. He had a collection of arrowheads at home, he said, and was intrigued when she told him about the pottery pieces she'd found on her Indian Hill. When he left her at the back door with a big wink and a "See you tomorrow," she smiled in return. Winnie was surprised to hear her humming a tune as she came into the kitchen.

Juliana saw a lot of Jason after that, though almost always the two of them were part of a small group, not alone together. Brother was obviously pleased that Juliana was interested in someone her own age. He posted a letter to Mamma, assuring her that she needn't worry any more about Juliana and Foster.

One afternoon Jason got up a group to walk to the Indian mound. Juliana took Margo along, for the little girl's heart was going to be crushed if she were left behind. Juliana had told her many Indian stories like the one about the Cherokee named Sequoyah who made up an alphabet for his people, and now reminded Margo to be quiet and listen so that maybe they'd learn something about the mound. First, they walked all the way around the bottom of it, Juliana in much awe of the size of it. It hadn't looked nearly so big at a distance.

"Wonder how many bones are in this thing," said Jason, poking a stick into a steep side.

"Oh, don't do that, Jason!" exclaimed a girl named Amy in horror. "This is a sacred place. Why, it may even be the place where Nacoochee and Sautee are buried."

"Well, they wouldn't be buried together," Jason declared, poking again.

"Why not? Who were they?" asked Juliana.

"You don't know about Nacoochee and Sautee? You must be a foreigner, a lowlander," said Jason, his eyes twinkling.

"So then—tell me who they were."

"Well, you know Yonah Mountain there," he said with a wave of his hand. "You can't see it from this angle, but at the top is a steep cliff on one side."

She nodded and clearly remembered viewing the mountain with Foster Kirk from his hilltop. He had said something about its being a lonely mountain apart from the others—like himself.

"Well, the story goes—" began one of the other boys, tossing a rock to see if he could make it go over the little gazebo.

"Wait, I'm telling this story," interrupted Jason. "What happened is this: Sautee, an Indian brave, fell in love with Nacoochee, a princess from another tribe. Of course they could only see each other on the sly. But one day they were caught, and Sautee was taken to the top of Yonah right up on the edge of that cliff and thrown off. Nacoochee was being held between two strong braves. But just as Sautee was hurled over the cliff, she broke away with a scream, and, running to the edge, jumped off after him."

"That's true love," sighed one of the girls.

"No, that's true stupidity," said Jason. "Just because one died didn't mean the other had to. What a waste!"

"Oh, Jason! For one who can tell such a good story, you are quite insensitive," replied the girl.

"And you don't think they're buried here?" asked Juliana.

"Would it make sense that the chief who had Yonah killed would then allow him to be buried with his daughter?"

Juliana considered, head cocked, chin resting on a curved forefinger.

"Yes, I think it would make sense," she said. "To an Indian, that is. Death changed everything. What was unforgivable in life was sweet and sentimental in view of the dark unknown."

The sun was behind the ridge now, shining like a red-gold border through the fringe of trees on top. A biting wind swooped down the valley, prodding the young people back toward the school. Jason gave Margo a ride and left Juliana to walk slightly apart from the others, hunching her shoulders against the cold.

She realized suddenly that everyone was staring at her, including Jason. But he quickly changed the mood by laughing at Juliana and breaking into a hard trot, with Margo's delighted peals piercing the chill air.

CHAPTER 9

IT HAD SNOWED SEVERAL times, but the light snows had stuck for only a few minutes. Juliana was as excited as Margo the day they awakened to find a thick blanket of white covering every twig and tree, and they bundled up and went out before breakfast, giggling at the crunching squeak of their shoes in the snow.

"See the rabbit tracks! And look, Margo, deer tracks! Oh, do be quiet, and maybe we will see a deer."

"How do you know who made these tracks?" whispered the little girl.

"I—just know. Because they're the shape of a deer's feet."

On the wooded slope above the house, Juliana turned to admire the scene. Hemlocks dropped graceful white-trimmed skirts; tree limbs were frosted with tiny ridges of snow, and back down the path of their sliding footprints stood the house and the school, black patches of roof showing here and there. Across on the next ridge, dark tree trunks and tips of spruce and pine peered out from the whiteness. The spire of the little church pointed up through snow-laden branches. In the stillness there was the occasional muffled snapping of a twig as snow weighted it to breaking point.

When Margo tugged at her hand, Juliana's eyes followed the child's pointed finger. A deer was observing them, large, luminous eyes wondering, black-tipped nose alert. Suddenly it spun around and was gone, a flash of white tail disappearing among the trees.

"That was a deer?" breathed Margo.

"That was a deer."

It was hard to concentrate in classes that day, for gazing out the windows. But particularly in Latin, where Brother was teacher, Juliana struggled to keep her mind on the subject. Brother had been very strict and had given her more work than anyone else, yet still she managed to keep a 93 average, and she had no intention of letting it slip. Her pride was at stake. She wanted to prove to him that she could do anything he assigned her.

When school was dismissed that afternoon, the path that wound by the boys' dormitory and on to Brother's house was black and wet with melted snow, but there was still plenty piled high on either side. Juliana and Jason walked ahead of a group of boys, Jason gallantly carrying Juliana's books for her. Intent on each other, the two didn't notice any unusual activity behind them until it was too late. Suddenly snowballs were pelting them, and shouts of glee rang out through the trees.

"Quick! Behind a bush!" ordered Jason. What followed was a battle Custer himself would have been proud of. As fast as Juliana made snowballs, Jason threw them. Ducking down behind the bush and scraping snow together as fast as she could, Juliana got only a few sprays of snow in her hair from the enemy fire. But during a lull, when Juliana lifted her head to peer over the top of the bush, a firm snowball connected with her face. She'd thought her nose and cheeks were completely numb, but realized with a sting that they were not.

"If you'll call a truce," she told Jason, rubbing her cheek, "I'll go get Winnie to fix us all some cocoa."

"Good deal. Hey, fellas! Juliana's inviting us for hot cocoa. Come on and behave yourselves, or Mr. Hamilton will put us all on probation."

Mr. Hamilton actually helped to prepare the cocoa. It took every little saucepan Winnie had to make enough of the steaming brew, and they had to take turns drinking because there weren't enough cups to go around. That seemed to make it all the more fun. When Juliana saw Brother hand Jason a cup and then laugh as he almost slid down on a puddle of melted snow, she felt a special warmth in her chest. Brother was not all stern authority. He just had a big dose of protectiveness where she was concerned, without as much of Henry's humor to go along with it.

As the snow melted, the waters of the Chattahoochee rose until there was no murmur and chuckle, only a loud roar. Juliana had developed a habit of visiting the river often. It was the next best thing to watching the water splash down her beloved Lorna Doone Slide. But heavy rains came to add to the snow melt until the whole valley was flooded. Even the Indian mound was almost covered. All that showed above the water was the little gazebo, and Juliana couldn't help wondering if Indians' bones might come floating to the top.

For two or three days the mailman could not make his rounds, but school went on as usual, for the small building was situated high on the hill and only the few commuting students had to be absent.

"If this weather doesn't break soon," said Winnie one day, "we're all going to go stir-crazy. Juliana, take Margo with you to see if the mailman got through today. You'll have to carry her across the bad places, but that won't hurt you, will it?"

Juliana thought she heard a touch of sarcasm in Winnie's voice. The implication that she had done little enough to earn her winter's lodging stung. She wanted to snap back that being there was not her idea and she didn't like it any better than Winnie, but she bit her lip and said only, "Come on, Margo, let's get buttoned up."

When she saw fresh hoof prints at the mailbox, Juliana pulled the door open in excitement. Maybe she would have a letter. Sometimes Byron wrote her; often Mamma did, and she had even heard several times from Grange.

"Let me see, let me see," demanded Margo beside her as Juliana sorted through the mail with awkward mittened fingers.

There was a letter to her from Mamma, mailed almost a week ago, several to Brother from different places, and one to Winnie from her mother; that would make her feel better. But she caught her breath at the sight of a small square envelope with the unmistakable handwriting of Foster Kirk. Margo was still demanding to see, but she heard her as from a distance. What could Foster have to say to her? How could he justify writing to her after all that had been said? A twist of anger burned through her as she studied the Atlanta postmark. Because of Foster Kirk she had been driven from her home, and now when things were beginning to improve between her and Brother, here was trouble again. Perhaps she could just hide the letter. But already Margo was standing on tiptoes to see, and her sharp eyes could not fail to notice the unusual script. Besides, that wasn't honest.

"I'm sorry, Margo, for being so pokey. Here, you hold the mail. Hold it with both hands, so it won't slide out and get all wet and muddy."

What could Foster be saying to her? He'd promised not to write or call until she was eighteen. Perhaps he was just letting her know how his exhibit had gone. She'd wanted very much to hear, but Grange had not mentioned it, and she didn't dare ask. Or he might be telling her he was getting married. In her imagination, the girls in Atlanta, decked out in their finery, were fantastically beautiful. Or what if something bad had happened? It was tempting to take the letter from Margo even now, and bribe her not to tell anyone about it. But as she glanced up, she saw Winnie looking out from the living room window with Peter in her arms. There was no use.

Juliana talked to Winnie about the letter, hoping that she would tell her to go ahead and read it. But Winnie didn't. "That's between you and your brother," she said adamantly. "I'm not getting into it."

Brother's forehead furrowed in a frown when he saw the letter. He gritted his teeth and started to tear it right down the middle.

"No, Brother, no!" pleaded Juliana. "You mustn't destroy it."

"And why not?"

"Because—well, surely he deserves to know that I received it. We must at least let him know it got here—or—or he'll send another."

"You'd like that, wouldn't you? And the next time you might read it."

"I could have read it this time—if I'd wanted to," said Juliana with painful evenness.

Brother looked at her bowed head and said remorsefully, "I suppose you could. Just the same, we can send the scoundrel the torn letter. I think that may be all he'll understand."

"No!" said Juliana with astonishing firmness, lifting her head, damp trickles shining on her cheeks. "Please, Brother, just write him a note yourself and tell him you didn't let me read it. Send it back the way it is. I wouldn't like it at all for him to get it back all torn up—as if I had done it in anger."

"I see. I was afraid of that." He turned the envelope around and around in his hands, walking toward the fire with it, then stopped and turned to Juliana again. "All right, I'll write a note. But if it happens again . . ."

"It won't happen again," she said quite positively, knowing that no one in the whole world could predict what Foster Kirk might do next.

Juliana was delighted when the Chattahoochee was back to normal. She took Margo with her to the mill and they stopped on the bridge to watch the water.

"Hear the water laughing?" asked Juliana.

"No, it's crying," said Margo.

"Depends on how you listen," said Juliana. "I'll drop in this weed, and we'll run around and watch it come out."

Margo clapped her hands when she saw the weed float by on the other side.

"I want to go over that bridge," she said, pointing to the swinging bridge.

"No, no, you might fall in. It swings you as you walk."

"You've walked on it?"

"Sure she has," said a deep voice, and there was Jason grinning and doffing a straw hat.

"Jason, did you follow us?" demanded Juliana.

"I just happened to be coming this way."

"To get flour? You bake bread in the dormitory?"

"No. As a matter of fact, a certain person I know has taught me to love this noisy old river, and I was coming to see it."

"That must be Judy," said Margo in surprise. "No one could love this river more than she does."

"Judy? Juliana? Maybe it was she, now that you mention it."

"Jason, you know it's against the school rules for

girls and boys to meet alone like this.''

His eyebrows shot up. ''Alone? We're not alone. Margo's here. You're somebody, aren't you, Margo?'' he asked, trying to curl a strand of straight blond hair around one finger.

''I sure am. I weigh as much as a sack of meal, a big one. My mamma said so.'' said Margo, pulling her hair free.

''See?'' Jason winked at Juliana and put a hand under one elbow, but she jerked away.

''What's gotten into you, Juliana?''

''Nothing. Come on and we'll get Winnie's flour. Don't you think it looks like rain?''

''No. That's just a wind cloud.''

''Are you sure?'' asked Juliana.

''Do I make mistakes?''

''Only occasionally,'' said Juliana with a laugh and a toss of her head.

They were almost back to Brother's house when the rain did come, roaring over the top of the ridge like a giant walking waterfall. They could smell it coming, and started running, Jason carrying Margo, Juliana carrying the flour. They pelted to the back door, laughing, out of breath, and drenched to the bone.

Winnie invited Jason to come in and, on Margo's request, they made popcorn.

''I hope you come lots of times,'' Margo told Jason, cuddling up to him on the window seat.

''I hope I can, too,'' said Jason, glancing at Juliana who made no response, but daintily nibbled a single kernel of popcorn.

Spring came to the Nacoochee Valley, and Juliana began to long for home in an urgent, painful way. Henry would be getting the fields ready for planting, talking long and patiently to his horses. Mamma would be planting her garden, and taking the mattresses out to sun. She could so well picture Sister and Byron starting out of a morning behind Maude, dear old Maude with the white blaze down her nose. She longed to be there, too.

The trilliums would be gone by now. The red and white clover would be blooming in the pastures, pink thistle brushes along the fences, and in the woods by a mossy tree she might find a clump of purple violets or Johnny-jump-ups.

When Brother did finally take them all home for a weekend, Juliana ran all over Clover Hill in jubilation. She stood on top of Indian Hill and hugged a big oak tree, laying her soft cheek against the rough, bumpy bark. She petted a new calf in the pasture and Henry said with his easy chuckle that no one but Juliana could get past a mamma cow to pet her young so easily. She sat on the porch steps, hugging and playing with Henry's new dog, Spring. And she devoured slice after slice of bread spread with rich yellow butter.

No one mentioned Foster Kirk at all. Finally, just before they left on Sunday afternoon, Juliana asked Byron about him as casually as she could. She and Byron had walked down to Lorna Doone Slide and spent a happy time talking about mutual friends. As casual as her question was, Byron still jerked his head up and looked at her with a sudden cloud disturbing his sunny face.

"Juliana, I know you liked Mr. Kirk. I did, too. I'm sorry he had to be unreasonable and expect to be able to court you. It just means we can't be friends with him, that's all."

"I only asked if you knew how he was—and his Aunt De and Beppo."

She could see Byron swallow, his big Adam's apple bobbing up and down. "I—I haven't seen him in a long time now," he faltered.

"He came to the house—*again?*"

"Yes, several times. He kept wanting your address, but Mamma wouldn't give it to him and finally one day—well *I* gave it to him."

"*You,* Byron?"

"Yes. He said he wanted to write to tell you good-by—that he was going to Florida."

"To Florida? Aunt De, too?"

"I think so. Although—he may be married by now. Grange said he saw him in Atlanta with a girl who lived next to Pinedale last summer."

Maureen. It would have to be Maureen Logan. With her brown hair and green eyes and her quick pouty temper. She knew with a dismal certainty that Maureen would be a terrible wife for Foster Kirk and that there was absolutely nothing she could do about it.

"Judy, I thought—what about Jason? Brother said you were liking him a lot."

"Why, of course I am," said Juliana, giving her long hair a toss over her shoulder. "But I don't think I'll miss him half as much when I leave Nacoochee as I've missed all of you at Clover Hill. I just belong at home. When I hear the roar of the river at night, I picture it with its grays and whites, its splashes and quiet places behind rocks. But then I think about Lorna Doone Slide."

"I know. I'll miss it, too, when I'm in college in North Carolina."

"You're not leaving this year?" Her voice was taut with sudden anxiety.

"No. Of course not. We have one more year to be in school together."

"Good! One more year to be children. Come on, Byron, I'll race you to the barn. Brother will be ready to leave by now."

CHAPTER 10

THAT SUMMER AT Clover Hill was marvelous beyond compare. Mamma's summer Sunday breakfasts were like banquets. She still cooked the way Papa liked, and it didn't matter to her if she had to get up before dawn to get it accomplished. Along with fried chicken (they ate the bony pieces for breakfast; saved the good pieces for dinner), there were sliced tomatoes, biscuits and gravy, fluffy scrambled eggs, and fried corn finely cut off the cob. Sunday dinner, except for the chicken, was prepared on Saturday. But Sunday breakfast was prepared straight from the garden to stove to table, steaming and unbearably enticing to anyone who might still be in bed. It was like a celebration every week.

Henry had bought a tractor. Mamma said he'd almost worn his farm record book out, figuring and refiguring all year, and scrimping along so that he could pay cash for the tractor even before the crops came in. He taught Juliana how to drive it, which she did fairly well, as long as she was in forward gear. Henry finally told her after some weeks that she might as well leave reverse alone before she landed down in the creek. Byron and Sister both teased her about the parasol she tied to herself to protect her complexion while she plowed, but she quietly commented that they could have freckles if they wanted them.

She kept expecting a letter from Jason. After all, he had asked for her address and told her he'd never forget her. Maybe she hadn't always been as kind to him as she should, but it was because she was so confused. Now that she wasn't seeing him anymore, she realized she cared a great deal about him. She wrote several letters to him, but of course wouldn't think of mailing one until she heard from him.

Brother accepted a call to be minister of a church in Linden, North Carolina, and in August he and Winnie bought an auto and moved. Margo hung onto Juliana's neck and sobbed, "Let me live with Judy! Let me live with Judy!" She was still crying at the back window, blond hair framing a red teary face as the car eased down around the bend and out of sight.

"It'll take 'em two days to get there," said Henry, rubbing his chin thoughtfully as he stared down the now empty road. "Brother thinks the road from here to Macoochee is bad, but I hear there are holes big enough to swim in between here and Asheville. And you'd do well to get stuck only two or three times."

"Oh, dear! Those poor children," sighed Mamma, wiping her nose.

Grange and Molly came once during the summer for

a weekend. Molly seemed much better and could get around so well that it seemed Grange never walked anywhere, even to Cold Spring and Ghost Den Ridge, that she was not right beside him. Somehow, Grange seemed more serious than before. He didn't tease Juliana as he always had since she was small enough to sit on his knee. It seemed that, if he talked to her at all, he cut his eyes toward Molly to see how she was taking it.

"Grange is one hen-pecked man," observed Henry after they left. "Doesn't the Bible say something about the misery of a man with a warring wife? You can count on it, Mamma, *this* son of yours is going to remain single all his days."

"I won't hold you to that, Henry," said Mamma. "Seems as if men tend to say things like that not long before they get married."

Richard planned his vacation from the bank in Clarkesville so that he could spend a week helping with the corn harvest at Clover Hill.

"Some life," commented Richard at the table one day. "Take a vacation to slave in the sun. We should have gone to Florida as our Clarkesville artist friend did. If he can afford to move to Florida when he has land debts stacked up to his chin, then I certainly can."

"Who are you talking about, Richard?" asked Mamma, laying down her fork.

"Foster Kirk. You asked me about him once, didn't you? Very upright guy, I'm sure, but I wouldn't want his debts. Somehow he always pays on his notes on schedule. Never once has he been late. But there's something fishy about a man laying up debts like that and moving to another state."

Juliana kept her head bowed over her plate, eating much more vigorously than her hunger demanded so that no one would notice she was interested in the topic of conversation. She wished Richard would say whether Foster took his family to Florida, but he never did. Somehow she felt very depressed thinking of the little gray houses with no smoke at the cottage chimney, no open door to the studio, no cats sunning on the porch and steps, no Delia Sweet in her sharp hairdo—and no Foster whistling, laughing, painting. And what was he doing in Florida, anyway? Maybe that's where Maureen wanted to live. Florida would suit her surely—a far-off romantic place. She could easily picture Maureen posing in one of those glamorous swimsuits from Rich's of Atlanta. She could see, too, Maureen's white poodle Serena running madly from a barking Beppo.

In the meantime the conversation had turned to Henry's tractor. Foster Kirk was only mentioned again in passing. Henry said, while stabbing the air with his fork for emphasis, that he would only buy things for which he could pay cash, whereupon Richard chuckled and said the banks would be in bad shape if everyone felt that way.

Later in the afternoon Juliana found a wild tiger lily in the woods above Mud Creek. She had taken the boys some water where they were plowing in Long Bottom and was walking back over Chestnut Hill instead of along the rocky, rutted road. She knelt beside the flower, looking closely at its orange petals sprinkled with spots like large flecks of black pepper. It was fascinating to study, but she wouldn't think of picking it, for then it couldn't reseed and there might never be any more. But on the way back to the house, she picked a handful of Indian pinks. There were always plenty of those.

All too soon the lazy days of summer passed. No more dangling her feet in the cool waters of Jenkins Branch, or hunting arrowheads on Indian Hill, or exploring Ghost Den Ridge with Byron on a Sunday afternoon, or sitting on the porch breaking beans. It was over, and it was time to go to school, but in Cornelia this time.

On the first day of school Henry found Maude dead in the barn when he went to hitch her to the buggy. Sister said Maude must have been tired of carrying them to school for so many years, and just decided she wouldn't go another time. It was the first time Juliana had seen Henry cry. He told Sister to take Black and Gray, and later that day, after he'd dug a deep grave and dragged Maude to it with the tractor, he walked to town and bought a new horse named John. Mamma told Juliana that she'd found Henry leaning on his shovel handle, sobbing by Maude's grave. "Henry couldn't come home for Papa's funeral," she said, "and, strange as it may seem, I think he was mourning Papa as well as Maude. You know, Maude was a special favorite of Papa's."

The cost of the new horse came close to wiping out the profit from the summer's crops. And John was a horse of a different caliber, not known for his obedience. He made the young people late to school many times because he would simply stop in the middle of the road and refuse to move. Henry could get him to do anything, but that was Henry, not Byron or Sister who drove to school each day.

In fact, Henry really seemed to prefer horses to people, anyway. On a winter evening, as Juliana and Byron sat at the table munching apples and studying Latin and poetry, Henry suddenly threw down his paper and stalked out the door. When he returned an hour or so later, Mamma asked where he'd been. "Down at the barn listening to the horses eat," he'd say. "Can't stand to listen to Byron and Judy chomping on apples."

Juliana's best friend Stella, who had at one time lived next to Clover Hill, but now lived in town, told her she hadn't really missed much the year before. The highlights of the school year had been Margie Whidden's Christmas party, where Buddy Crane had broken his nose running into a door facing while playing Blindman's Bluff, and the school play in which Miss Shannon, the language teacher, ended up playing Juliet because Elizabeth Miller became mysteriously ill at the last minute.

"I think it was because Spike Henderson was Romeo," she confided. "Now that you're back, maybe Spike won't win all the spelling bees. It has been so boring. And now I want to hear all about what happened. Why did you go off to school like that?" Stella's face was full of anticipation for the story she'd been longing to hear.

But Juliana disappointed her. All she would say was that Mamma wanted her to go live with Brother for a while, that Nacoochee was a beautiful place (Did she know that Nacoochee meant "Evening Star"?), and that she'd learned a new Indian legend, walked a swinging bridge, and had a boyfriend named Jason. Stella had heard rumors about the artist in Clarkesville, and tried to pry something out of Juliana. But best friend or not, Stella could not be trusted with the intricacies of that relationship with Foster Kirk. All Juliana would ever admit was that he was a friend of the family and that he had painted her portrait which she showed her awed friend when she came to visit. "I wish an artist would do my portrait," Stella said dreamily.

A little later when the girls sat down to a cup of tea, Stella leaned forward eagerly, ready to hear about Jason.

"Is he very handsome? Does he like the outdoors? Did he ask you to marry him?"

Juliana laughed so that she jostled tea out of her cup and onto Mamma's lace tablecloth. "Stella Adams! I don't plan to marry anyone for at least ten years!" she exclaimed.

"But did he ask you?"

"No. Not exactly."

"Oh, how terribly romantic. I do wish I were pretty and smart like you, and someone would ask me."

"Stella, I told you he *didn't* ask me. And you *are* pretty and smart. Why, with those enchanting curls in front of your ears, you look just like a model."

"Do I *really?*"

Mamma, hearing the girls' chatter, sighed happily. It was so good to have Juliana home to stay.

Juliana soon found it was no small thing to compete against Spike Henderson who had moved the year before from Roanoke, Virginia, and already considered himself at the top of his class. Even when she beat him in algebra competitions and essay contests, Juliana knew that it was a very close thing, and she couldn't help feeling sorry for him as she watched the frustration grow in his sober, never-smiling face. All the same, she had no intention of doing any less than her best.

Juliana enrolled in an elocution class with Byron. Sister also wanted her to take piano again, but Juliana stubbornly refused, remembering the wretched hours of practicing years before. In elocution she and Byron memorized many poems, as well as writing and delivering speeches. They practiced on old stubborn John, the horse, as well as Sister, who were forced to listen to long recitations on the road back and forth to school.

One day on the way home Byron became more enthusiastic than usual as he recited "Recessional" by Rudyard Kipling. He stood in the buggy and waved his arms in emphasis to trees as they passed, exactly as if the trees were grand ladies and gentlemen in a lecture hall. Juliana and Sister both developed the silly giggles over Byron's stern formality, but Sister, being a teacher with a serious image to protect, tried to be sedate when she saw a buggy approaching. She commanded Byron to sit down, then when he wouldn't, she tried to pull him down with one hand. But he was in a playful mood and was thoroughly enjoying himself, forgetful of all his shyness.

As the approaching buggy rattled closer and closer, Sister was able to recognize an old German peddler who had been to the house many times. She sighed with relief, glad that it was not the minister or, worse still, the school principal, and she prepared to give Kurt a friendly nod. But John was very tired of all this nonsense, the wobbling of the buggy as Byron balanced like an inexperienced politician, the awkward handling of the reins, and, above all, the outrageous recitation in full voice. John took matters under his own control as, with a sudden lurch, he plunged forward at full speed.

Byron barely escaped falling out the back as Juliana hung onto him, her books and papers falling to the floor or scattering to the winds. Sister was pulling back on the reins as hard as she could, but to no avail. John's ears were turned back, his neck arched defiantly, as he galloped on. Kurt, the peddler, turned a startled white face toward them just before his own horse, a rib-showing, dull-haired black, broke into his own sudden gallop, spilling some bottles and boxes out the back.

All three young people were holding their sides in helpless laughter when John finally stopped with a loud snort in front of the barn door.

"We didn't hurt John." Byron was defensive when Henry accused him of mistreating the animal. "We were only reciting poetry. I can't help it if he's a temperamental creature."

"Ought to have better sense than to torture him like that," said Henry sourly, giving John an affectionate slap and allowing the horse to rub his head up and down on his shirt, smearing it with sweaty grime.

"I wonder if the poor peddler retrieved his little bottles and boxes," said Juliana, trying to straighten out the crimped edges of her Latin book.

"We would have helped him if we could have stopped John," said Sister. "Henry, you know the German peddler who's been here several times? Mamma's bought vanilla from him before."

"So that's who drove up awhile back," said Henry, leading John into the barn. "I heard the chickens making a big to-do, and Spring ran up there barking. But by the time I got there, there was nothing but buggy tracks left. Well, I won't worry about missing him. I didn't want any vanilla or tonic, although the poor cuss could use some business, I'm sure. A lot of people around here are suspicious of him because he's German. They're still trying to keep the war alive, I guess."

"Funny. I didn't see Mamma at all when we came by," said Byron. "I know she must have been startled. Or has she gone somewhere?"

"Gone to the Davises," answered Henry. "Mrs. Davis's daughter Laura is having her baby, I reckon. Blake came to get Mamma."

"Good old Blake," said Juliana. "I wonder what will ever become of him. I wish . . ."

"I know," said Sister. "you always thought he could have learned to read and write if someone had known how to teach him. Wonder what made him the way he is, anyway. I hope Laura's baby is all right."

"Oh, you girls! Always worrying about things you can do nothing about. Now get out of my way, and let me soothe this poor horse. You could do well to worry about *him* now and then."

"Henry, you are impossible!" exclaimed Sister over her shoulder as the girls left the barn. Byron stayed behind to appease his brother.

As they approached the house, Juliana paused in the path. "You know, Sister, I haven't seen the Davises very much since I've been back home. I guess I've been too busy. And Blake hasn't teased me lately. I think—let's walk over there. Want to?"

"I'd like to. I haven't seen Laura since she moved to Demorest. But I'd better start supper. Mamma may not be home for a long time. You know how slow these—things—can be. Let me take your books, and *you* go."

The Davises' house was small and unpainted, with lots of room under the house for chickens to take dust baths. Juliana remembered with a shudder the time when she and some other children had been playing hide-and-seek, and she had hidden behind one of the pillars under the house. She'd been so quiet and had thought no one had any idea where she was when, suddenly, hands covered her eyes from behind and clamped tight. In the sudden darkness she'd panicked and screamed, then heard the sniveling, snickering sound that only Blake could make.

Now she could see that old broken chairs, a lawn-mower, and other things had been packed under the house. The low-slanting sun rays made grotesque shadows of handles, rungs, and wheels. As her steps crunched in the fresh, fallen leaves a dog ran down from the porch barking, and immediately Blake's bulky body appeared at the door, his face breaking into smiles at sight of Juliana. She received his hug as she always had when they were children.

"How is Laura, Blake?"

"She's bad. Babies are bad."

"Oh, no, not the babies themselves! Just the pain. I'm sure Laura will be all right. Just think, Blake, you'll be an uncle!" She laughed over her shoulder at him as she stepped into the house. Roger and Ben Davis rose to greet her, obviously pleased to have a fresh face and voice to break the monotony. Mamma, hearing her voice, stepped out of the bedroom where Laura lay. Her hair was falling from the pins, and her cheeks sagged.

"Juliana, I'm glad you're here. You need to cook some supper for these folks. Maybe the boys can show you where things are in the kitchen. You can make some bread and gravy or a stew or something. But be sure and keep the kettle of water hot."

"But, Mamma, I—"

"Yes, you can do it, Juliana," she said firmly. "Boys, see to it she finds what she needs. I think—it won't be long now." She turned quickly as there was a wrenching scream from the bedroom.

Blake clapped his hands over his ears and closed his eyes tightly almost as if he were the one in pain.

Juliana's heart thudded against her ribs, and she licked her lips that had suddenly gone dry. "All right," she said, trying to sound steady and controlled, "show me where your skillet is, and where you keep your eggs."

Juliana gained more and more confidence as she

moved about the kitchen—straining the evening milk, breaking eggs in a bowl, and turning thick slices of bacon as they sputtered in the skillet. *What would Jason think of me preparing supper all by myself for three grown men?* she wondered. *Or Foster?* She paused in her vigorous stirring of eggs. *Foster. Where is he now? Is Maureen kind to him?* She gave a little scream as big arms closed around her from behind.

"Blake Davis, you almost made me spill this bowl of eggs. Now don't do that!" She squirmed to extricate herself from his hold, but found she was quite powerless. "Roger! Ben! Make Blake let me go so I can finish your supper!" she commanded sternly.

Blake suddenly dropped his arms, and her shoulders sagged in relief.

"Don't you like me any more, Miss Juliana?" he asked in a hurt tone.

"Of course I do. That's why I'm making supper for you," she said briskly. "Now sit down like a good boy and wait till I call you."

The boys were eating when the baby was born, a fine healthy baby girl. "It's a shame Laura's husband was out west when his first child was born," said Mamma as she and Juliana walked home in the moonlight.

"Why is he out west?"

"Seeking better things. People are becoming more and more dissatisfied living the way they always have. I declare, it looks as if they would realize how good things are at home without roaming so far away. But then, it's really not a new urge—to wander, I mean.

Your papa had it, too. He would have moved to south Georgia in a minute if his deal had worked out."

"Mamma, you're tired and you're getting out of breath. Better just walk and not talk, don't you think? The stars are out and the moonlight is so pretty—like a peaceful blessing on our trees and the roof of our house. A beautiful night for a baby to be born."

"Yes. A fine baby, too," said Mamma. Then, lowering her voice, she added sadly, "I hope she's not like Blake."

Juliana looked behind her with a sudden nameless fear. She was glad when they were again safe at Clover Hill.

Just before Thanksgiving the Davises had a corn shucking. That was when Henry met Martha Brady and began dressing up and riding off in the buggy behind John for long rides on Saturday afternoons. And that's when Juliana began really to fear Blake Davis, for whom she'd felt only sympathy all her life. The boy had never been quite right and had never gone to school, but everyone considered him harmless, just a pitiful nitwit who was good for nothing but slopping pigs and killing chickens.

At the corn shucking Juliana noticed Blake watching her every move, and his eyes didn't stay on her hands shucking corn or on her face, either. He kept looking disturbingly at a point in between, until she looked several times to see if her sweater had popped a button or if she'd spilled some of Mrs. Davis's barbecue sauce down her front.

Blake handled his sister's tiny baby with tender

care, his big hands making a cradle for the little one as he hauled her around to all the shuckers, bragging on her beauty. Stella, shucking next to Juliana, nudged her with an elbow after Blake had moved on. "I'm glad I'm living in town," she said. "That boy scares me. It's his eyes."

The two girls entered into the shucking contest with spirit and, though neither of them won in the girls' division, they certainly made it tough for Martha Brady. Juliana had seen Henry talking to the dark-haired girl early in the day and was glad her lonely brother was enjoying a little well-deserved diversion. But as things had progressed, Juliana had become almost jealous, for Henry had not noticed her as he usually did. After the final corn shucking contest, as she and Stella stood by the wide barn door, Henry ambled by and pulled a lock of Juliana's hair, a familiar gesture, accompanied by a one-sided grin. Things hand't changed after all.

After the corn shucking Juliana could not feel comfortable when she saw Blake Davis, even at a distance. She didn't trust the wandering look in his eyes.

One evening she was hurrying toward home, having studied late at Stella's. She'd promised to be home before dark, and now the shadows were long and the blackness of night crept in toward the road. When she heard the clip-clop of horses' hooves, she glanced over her shoulder, and, seeing Mrs. Davis and Blake, she walked even faster. But the buggy slowed as it came up behind her, and Blake jumped down, his big red face not far from hers as he announced, "We take you home, Miss Juliana."

Involuntarily she sprang back from him, and stammered, "I-I-I'm in a hurry."

"So let us give you a ride, dear," said Mrs. Davis pleasantly, and Blake grinned at her, his eyes traveling swiftly down her brown coat to her stockinged ankles and back up again.

"No—no, thank you," she said and, with her throat tight with unnamed fear, she turned and walked on again, leaving Blake looking after her. Soon the buggy passed her again, and for Mrs. Davis's sake, she lifted one hand in a little wave, but she would not look up.

"You little goose," Mamma said to Juliana when she heard about it. "To tell our good neighbor you were in too big a hurry for a ride!"

She didn't know how to explain to Mamma how she felt about Blake. To Mamma he was still the helpless child who played silly tricks. And maybe he was. Maybe, thought Juliana, he was as harmless as ever.

CHAPTER 11

WHEN BYRON GRADUATED at the top of his class in June, no one was more delighted than Juliana. She swelled with pride until she felt like bursting as he gave his speech, which was an oration that did credit to the long hours and miles of recitation. She smiled to herself, remembering how Byron had once been so shy he wouldn't even go to Foster Kirk's without her, and now he was speaking boldly before a crowd and planning to go off to Davidson College in North Carolina in the fall.

The family wasn't really surprised that Byron was valedictorian.

"After all," said Henry grumpily, "anybody who drives a tractor with a book in one hand should be voratorian—or whatever you call it."

"Has a girl ever been valedictorian?" Juliana asked as she and Sister washed the supper dishes.

Sister looked at her quickly, her face alert, her eyes

searching her younger sister's carefully curtained expression. She squeezed out the dishrag and walked over to the stove where she began to wipe the white enamel on the warming closet doors.

"Of course there have." She paused significantly. "And there will be again."

Juliana never understood what happened to the summer after Byron's graduation. Maybe it was knowing that he would soon be leaving that made the green-gold days fly by so quickly, though she longed to hug each one tightly to her heart. They did so many things for the last time—picked apples in the orchard, took long strolls on Indian Hill, raced to see who could find the largest number of brown thrashers' nests, and, of course, made one last tearful visit to Lorna Doone Slide.

When the day came to see Byron off to college, Juliana thought her heart would break. She knew a precious part of her girlhood had ended. The falling leaves echoed her loss, until suddenly it was winter, with only her schoolwork and an occasional letter from Byron to remind her that she must move resolutely ahead, following all the bends in the road.

On a cold, windy day in December, Sister and Juliana started toward the stable in town where John stayed while they were in school. Juliana was looking forward to telling Sister all that Miss Shannon had told her recently about the scholarship being offered by an elderly gentleman in the community. She shifted her books to the other arm and dug in her coat pocket for two apple cores she'd saved for John. But John was in a bad mood. He refused Juliana's treat, slung his head when they tried to harness him, even bared his teeth at Sister.

When he planted himself solidly with back hooves in the stall door, Juliana thought they must give up, but Sister sent her up in the loft to try to drop the harness over his head. John tossed his head violently and the harness fell into a pile of fresh manure. The girls shivered and surveyed the situation. They would have to go past John's kicking heels in order to retrieve the harness. When Juliana said, "Let's just walk," Sister didn't argue.

The road had not thawed all day and now purple shadows fell across white patches in the crusty red ruts. The girls' legs felt wooden up to their knees, and they stumbled over frozen clods of clay. Their fingers ached in permanent curved positions around their books, the woolen mittens affording little relief from the penetrating cold. But even with the wind grabbing their words and threatening to freeze their very teeth, Juliana was eager to tell Sister about the scholarship.

"Miss Shannon thinks I have a chance for it, even though Spike Henderson has an edge on me right now."

"And the scholarship would pay your tuition for a whole year? At what college?"

"Any one I choose. Oh, Sister, you know I won't get it! And I don't want to go away from home again anyway. But it's so exciting to try—just to see if I can do it!"

"Of course you can do it!" exclaimed Sister, hugging her books tighter for warmth, and walking faster. "Since I'm going to North Carolina to teach next year, you could go to Flora McDonald in Red Springs. It's a good college for girls. We could get together at Brother's for the holidays, you and Byron and me. Wouldn't that be fun!"

"But then Mamma and Henry . . ."

"They could come, too. They could ride up on the train."

Juliana pulled her scarf across her nose for a minute's reprieve from the biting wind. She knew she couldn't leave Clover Hill again, couldn't bear to go through that terrible homesickness, but—a scholarship that she could earn herself! She had the application with her and would fill it out that night. She had already looked it over, and the only thing that worried her now was what to write on the line that asked what career she planned to pursue.

The girls scooped out the mail as they went by the box, but didn't stop to see to whom the letters were addressed. Mamma met them on the porch, pulling them in, and closing the door against the wind. The creases between her eyes were deep as she listened to John's latest escapade. At the same time she settled them in chairs in front of the open oven door, and set a pan of warm water on a stool between them for their icy hands. Juliana sniffed appreciatively at the warm smell of fresh bread, then felt a trickle run from her thawing nose. Mamma pulled a handkerchief out of her bosom and handed it to her.

"You girls will catch your death this way," she fussed. "Papa would have already had you boarding for the winter in Cornelia, but it's so lonesome here without you."

"Oh, we're all right, Mamma!" said Juliana. "We don't want to go and board again, do we, Sister? Why don't you see what's in the mail?"

There was a letter from Grange which Mamma read to them. It was filled with the usual hilarious descriptions of people at work, but there was a note of concern, too. "I know you always take in anyone who needs a night's rest, because that's how I got to know you myself. But these times can be dangerous, and I wish you would be careful. The Ku Klux Klan has been reorganized, and they're threatening anyone who even helps a German or Jew." He barely mentioned Molly—only to say that she was not very well and maybe spring would perk her up.

"Poor Grange," sighed Mamma, folding the letter, "I'm afraid Molly will never be well."

"And what about the Ku Klux Klan, Mamma?" asked Sister.

Juliana noticed the deep valleys running from Mamma's nose down by her mouth. "I can't believe they'd bother us, but we must be alert, and we *must not* be out after dark," she said, creasing Grange's letter between her fingers.

There were heavy footsteps on the porch, and a rush of cold air as Henry let himself in. He came directly to the stove, holding his fingers over the heat, and stamping his feet to bring them back to life. Juliana looked up at his face, lined already with wind and sun wrinkles and so red now, his lips chapped and cracked.

"I'll make you some coffee, Henry," she said, getting to her feet.

He turned blue eyes on her, then on Sister who had slid her feet into the oven and was blissfully soaking up the heat. "Where's John?" he asked.

"We couldn't get him hitched up," said Juliana. "We tried and tried, but it was so cold we finally gave up."

Henry looked first astonished, then angry, and finally bewildered as he stood there warming himself, glancing out the window at the trees blowing in the wind. It would soon be dark, and threatened to be one of the coldest nights of the year.

"I'm sorry, Henry," said Juliana helplessly.

"We'll walk in the morning," said Sister, "and by tomorrow afternoon John will be glad to come home."

Henry didn't answer. He just jammed his stocking hat back down over his ears, turned the collar up on his old army coat, and went out the door, closing it firmly behind him.

"Supper will be ready soon!" Mamma called after him, but only the wind answered.

"He's going to walk to town and get him!" exclaimed Juliana, watching from a window.

"I told him we'd get him tomorrow!" said Sister. "John would be all right in that stable."

"But he didn't have supper, did he?" asked Mamma. "And you know Henry. He won't eat himself unless his horses are cared for first. I just hope . . . but I know Henry will be fine."

They knew she was thinking of the Ku Klux Klan.

Mamma swished her hand around in the washtub of hominy. It was the third washing. Maybe one more would take out the bitterness of the oak ash, and she would be through. All day since right after breakfast, she'd cooked the shelled corn until it was the color of wheat, each kernel puffy and tender. Now for an hour she'd been washing it, standing by the wash bench out back. Every now and then she found a bad kernel she had missed in her pre-cooking scrutiny, and she threw it to a clutch of chickens that milled around her expectantly.

Scooping the last of the corn into a clean tub of water, she straightened up, wiped her chapped hands on her apron, and rubbed a place in the small of her back. She looked toward the west at the setting sun, outlining a tree full of early starlings that looked like French knots embroidered against the sky. Then she looked anxiously toward the driveway. It was time Juliana was home. This business of staying in town to study with Stella had gotten to be too much of a habit lately. The child was studying herself to death and to what end? She couldn't get that scholarship, and even if she did, what good would it do her to have one year of college when she couldn't have any more? There was no money to keep her there.

She bent toward her work again. Henry had studied and figured late into the night over his farm record book, and she guessed he was wanting to get married and build a house. But there wasn't any cash available for him or for Juliana, and no prospects of any. Besides, what would Juliana do with a college education? The girl had a headful of dreams that she guarded as carefully as a miner would his gold nuggets. Mamma smiled to herself and said out loud, "If that waterfall could talk, maybe I'd learn what's going on in my little girl's head.''

She glanced up again, feeling the chill as the sun's rays disappeared completely. ''Where is that child?'' she wondered, and she couldn't help thinking about her own encounter recently with the Ku Klux Klan.

She'd been on her way home from nursing the little Davis grandbaby who had the croup. It was already dark when she started home, and she'd given old John the reins and let her mind shift into restful neutral, though she was jostled hither and fro on the rough road.

Suddenly without warning she was surrounded by the horsemen in their white capes and black hoods, all silent, all holding lanterns. She tightened the reins and was glad John just stopped and didn't snort and rear.

''Just what do you want?'' she demanded, surprised that her voice didn't shake.

At first no one had answered. She remembered her arms prickling, how frightened she'd been of their silence, their ominous masked silence.

Then one had come forward, and, stopping directly in front of her, his lantern blinding her, he'd spoken. ''We know you've been harboring foreigners on your farm.''

At first she couldn't think what foreigner they could mean, then she'd laughed in relief, ''Oh, you must mean that poor old German peddler. You can't possibly care if I buy vanilla from a man who's trying to make a living, and maybe give him a bite to eat and a place to sleep. *You* would want the same under similar circumstances.'' There had been that awful silence again. Then she'd felt anger surging inside of her, and it hadn't mattered what she said. "There are potholes in this road that need to be fixed, and all you can do is get out in the dark and plague people who are trying to live peaceably. If you want to do something, why don't you fix this road?"

There was a menacing growl from the Klan figures which moved in to envelope her. Then the spokesman held up one hand and the low rumbling stopped abruptly.

"Madam!" he said. "It shall be done!"

She'd sat there, stunned, watching them ride off, the shadows of their capes and masks thrown up against the blackness of the woods in the lantern light.

Now she wondered if those men were out tonight, with Juliana alone and on foot along the road. She knew Juliana was more afraid of Blake Davis than she was of the Klan, but surely that fear was unfounded. All the Hamiltons had cared for Blake since he was in diapers, and he'd always been so lovable and kind. Still, Juliana was not one to complain, and *she* felt there was something to fear. Mamma decided that when Juliana got home, she would tell her she just must not study at Stella's unless she were going to spend the night.

Juliana herself was not particularly concerned as she started home from Stella's house. She knew she had stayed too late again, but she'd gotten so much done. Stella was as interested in her winning the scholarship as she was. In fact, she would have given up before now if it hadn't been for Stella and Sister—and Miss Shannon. Miss Shannon had told her only today that she felt Juliana had some special contribution to make to the world and that she would do all she could to help her. Thinking of it now, Juliana did a little skip in the road and lightly hummed a tune.

A rabbit hopped into the road in front of her, and she stopped to watch it sitting there, a snug hump of fur with perky, pricked ears. A twig snapped, and the bunny jumped on across the road. As Juliana started on, she thought she heard footsteps in the woods beside the road. But when she stopped, she heard nothing and decided it was her imagination. Realizing how dark it had gotten, and that Mamma would be worried, she hurried along.

A scurry of dry leaves blew into the road like so many biddies following a mother hen. At the same moment Juliana heard someone cough. It could only be a cough. There was no other sound it could be. Her heart hammered in her chest, and her knees felt suddenly weak as she looked behind her and realized what a long, lonely stretch of road it was. There wasn't a glimmer of light from a house or cottage anywhere in sight, only the dusky road, and the dark woods shouldering close. Licking dry lips, she started on, willing herself to think about the scholarship and thus forget her fear until she was safely home.

She was totally unprepared to defend herself against the big shape that suddenly extricated itself from the dark anonymity of the woods and engulfed her in arms that were like a steel trap. The hard corners of her books dug into her soft flesh and, with terror, she heard Blake Davis's voice shrilling in exultation, "I got you! I got you now, Miss Juliana!"

The more she struggled, the harder he held her until she could barely breathe. His hot breath was close and heavy with the nauseating smell of onions. In desperation she drew back one foot and kicked his shin as hard as she could. He let out a yowl and let go of her. Her books still hugged to her chest, she started running, but for all her speed he was right there, his big hands grasping her arms, pulling her against him. "I will not let you go, Juliana. You're mine," he cooed. "I've waited, oh so long, and you won't leave me now. I'll take you where no one will ever find you and we'll be happy. Just you and me."

It was dark now. She couldn't see his face, even if she dared to look up. But she must think of something to say that would change his mind. How could she bribe him? *Oh, God, help me,* she prayed, *Help me be calm like Mamma with the KKK's. Help me think of something wise to say.*

"If you'll take me home, Blake, I'll fix you a wonderful big supper," Juliana said in the soothing tone his mother used with him. She felt him thinking about it. He loved to eat. "Maybe some sausage and eggs —and—and—hot biscuits with butter," she continued. He was very quiet, his breathing heavy and horrible, but otherwise quiet. He just stood there, holding her in a frozen vise.

Then suddenly he thrust her from him, his hands gripping bruisingly into her arms.

"You think you can bribe me," he snarled. "Don't try that, Juliana. Don't try it!"

He shook her then and she dropped her books and began to beat against him with her fists. But his grip on her arms was so hard that it did no good, and he laughed cruelly.

"I've been waiting for this and you're not getting away from me anymore," he said.

Neither of them noticed the sound of a car engine until it was bearing down just beyond the turn. Blake tried then to jump the ditch with her and get out of sight, but she struggled and kicked and managed to hold her ground. Car lights flooded them, illuminating the grim tableau. A motor roared and the car stopped within a foot of them, but Blake hung on still, his breathing hard and fast.

"They can't make me let you go. They can't make me!" he was saying over and over, even as a fist connected abruptly with the side of his chin.

"Juliana, get in the car!" yelled Foster Kirk as he dealt Blake another blow, this time knocking him into the ditch.

Juliana stood by the car, but would not get in. She shuddered at the grunts and groans of the men and the sickening thuds of flesh on flesh. It looked as if Blake had given up and was just letting Mr. Kirk pound him mercilessly.

"Don't hurt him!" she cried out. "He—he—didn't know what he was doing!"

But no sooner were the words out of her mouth than she saw Foster lift big Blake by his overalls and hurl him across the ditch. Foster leapt after him and grabbed hold of him as if he wanted to pick him up just to beat him down again.

Juliana screamed, "Don't hurt him!" and was relieved when Foster reluctantly turned away from the shadowy heap.

As Foster strode back into the full lights of the car, she saw the ugly gash over one eyebrow and blood running from his nose. But he stopped anything she might have said by snapping, "I said get in!"

"But—we can't just leave him there."

"What do you suggest we do—take him to your house?"

"No, but he lives nearby . . ."

"He'll get home. He isn't out for long. Now get in before I pick you up and put you in!"

Seeing her shaking uncontrollably, he pulled off his coat and placed it around her, his strong hands gentle as he adjusted it to her shoulders. It was a leather coat and smelled just like him, rugged and woodsy. She pulled it close around her, and as they bumped along, stole a glance at his face. It was too dark to see anything but the barest outline of his jutting chin. Even so, she could feel his anger like a live force between them. It terrified her at the same time that it comforted her in a way she couldn't understand.

"He—he's a nitwit," she blurted out now by way of explanation. "He's never hurt anybody before."

A muscle worked in his jaw, and, after a moment, he said, "I could have killed him. When I saw him attacking you, it unleashed every ounce of anger in me. You were one plucky firebrand, though," he added with a chuckle as he turned into Clover Hill.

A flood of relief swept over her—he didn't blame her! Suddenly the full impact of the shame and fear hit her and she began to cry, pressing her knuckles hard against her mouth.

"Are you all right, Juliana? Did he hurt you?" asked Foster, slowing the car. His voice was so instantly tender that her tears flowed faster.

"It's just—just that—I've lost all my books," she stammered, knowing full well that wasn't why she was crying.

"You were just getting home from school?" he asked in a shocked tone.

"I was studying at my friend Stella's."

After a minute's silence he said between his teeth, "Don't worry, I'll get the books for you. But why in the name of thunder would you have to study so late?"

They were parked now in front of the house. She looked helplessly at his dark profile and could not answer. Then Mamma and Henry were running out with Sister right behind them. Juliana slid out of the coat and was fumbling to open the door when Foster, who had come around the car with Spring leaping and barking around his feet, flung the door open for her and reached in to help her out. Unaccountably she refused his hand and stood by herself.

"What's this?" demanded Henry harshly, recognizing Foster Kirk and seeing Juliana looking scared and rumpled.

"I found Juliana—" began Foster, then looked down at her drooping head. "I'll let her tell you," he said in a tightly controlled voice. "And I hope you'll realize she shouldn't be out so late. I hate to think what might have happened if I hadn't come along."

"Now just a minute, sir," said Henry, stepping forward belligerently.

"That's all right, I'm leaving," said Foster, turning on his heel. "But, remember, I'm not the real enemy," he flung over his shoulder. He raced his motor, turned the car around, and rocked off down the driveway, leaving them in total darkness.

"Juliana?" asked Mamma, an arm around her trembling shoulders. "The Ku Klux Klan?"

"No, Mamma. Blake Davis."

The next morning Juliana found her books stacked in the porch chair by the front door. She didn't know when he had put them there, but she was sure Foster had left them. Where was he today? And why had he been on Mud Creek Road last night? He had not explained, and now she was unlikely to see him again.

Mrs. Davis came over in the afternoon and sat at the dining table, weeping into a cup of strong coffee. "Don't tell on my poor Blake," she begged over and over, with Mamma assuring her all the time that she wouldn't. "I don't know what made him do it. He's not like that. You know yourself, Mrs. Hamilton, he's gentle as a kitten. If it'd been anyone else but you folk, I wouldn't believe it. I'd think it was a trick. But the bruises on Juliana's poor white arms—and her word, too, that I've always trusted. Oh, if only Mr. Davis hadn't left me. How can I bear this all alone?"

"You're not alone. That's what Christian friends are for," said Mamma, standing behind the distraught woman, gently massaging her shoulders. "We would have come last night, but you said Blake was home and you were busy treating his wounds. By the way, he is all right, isn't he? I suppose he walked home?"

"No." Mrs. Davis shuddered in a spasm of fresh sobs. "*He* brought him—that man—the same one who beat him up."

"Foster Kirk?" asked Mamma in surprise, looking quickly at Juliana whose blond head jerked up from her book.

"Yes, him. I begged him not to tell, but he never promised. Just brought my boy in and got him on the bed. He asked if he could help, and when I said no, he left. My boy may go to jail . . ." she wailed.

"He will not!" declared Juliana. "I won't testify against him."

For weeks they expected any day to have a visit from the sheriff, but no one ever came. Juliana kept her bruises well covered with long sleeves, and when the lesions were only pale green, she looked at them and wondered if the whole ordeal had only been a terrible nightmare. She had written to Foster Kirk and begged him not to tell anyone about Blake, assuring him that Mrs. Davis and her other sons were watching him closely now and would keep him out of trouble. But she never had an answer from him. It was as if he'd never been back, as if she'd imagined it all. Finally she stopped watching all the cars in town as if she might see him and settled back into her rigid study schedule, working even harder to make up for lost time, but making sure she never stayed late at Stella's except to spend the night.

One day Mamma found the portrait of Juliana hidden behind the phonograph. Upon questioning Henry and learning that he had done it, she chided him soundly.

"I don't want to be reminded of that man," grumbled Henry. "I wish he'd stay in Florida and mind his own business."

"Henry, I'm surprised at you! You know Juliana could have been seriously injured if Foster hadn't rescued her."

Henry grunted something under his breath and strode out of the house, on his way to the barn to talk to the horses.

CHAPTER 12

ON JUNE 1 THERE WAS a general buzz of excitement in all the rooms at Cornelia High, but particularly in the room where the seniors awaited the news from a panel of teachers as to who would be valedictorian and salutatorian, and this year, even more interesting, who would be the recipient of the Walter K. Durden Scholarship. The teachers had been closeted in the principal's office across the hall for more than an hour now.

"It must be the decision about the scholarship that's taking so long," said Stella nervously, glancing at Juliana's pale face with the flushed spots of excitement on her cheeks.

"They just want to make us sweat," said Spike Henderson, pacing with agitation in the hot room. He talked so confidently yet he was nervous, too, thought Juliana, or he wouldn't be walking back and forth so. Poor Spike, he really wanted that scholarship and he would probably put it to better use than she. She almost wished she could remove her application, but it was too late now. And anyway she really wanted to go to college, to go on learning.

Juliana's supporters clustered around her. She wished they would leave her alone, but she didn't want to hurt their feelings. She was glad when a spitball fight erupted, for she managed to stay in her desk and not get involved. That way she could think what she might do next, now that school was over.

Whether she won or not, she felt she had made a good showing. If Spike did win, he certainly hadn't had it easy. The competition had been keen. All those late nights by the kerosene lamps, the many afternoons that she'd carried her books with her to study by Jenkins Branch, the tests, the spelling bees, the drills in French—all of it was worth it, no matter what.

Once she'd thought she would be a teacher like Sister, but now she wasn't sure. She just knew she still wanted to learn. There was more knowledge than she'd even scratched, and she wasn't ready to stop now. And somewhere there was a special task for her. She had not been born just to be, but to do.

She started in her seat as someone shouted, "Here they come! Into your desks!" Instantly the tension was back. Her hands were sticky and her heart thumped hard. No matter how she might rationalize, she wanted to be the top student, and she wanted that scholarship. There would have been no fun in trying so hard if there hadn't been that hope.

The principal, whose thin hair was graying, was a little on the plump side. On this afternoon, as he stood before the miraculously quiet seniors, he mopped the sweat from his face with a handkerchief, then stuck it in his pocket so he could hold a half-sheet of paper with both hands. He cleared his throat, folded and unfolded the paper, and finally, over the drumming of a bee trying to get out the top of one of the tall windows, he began to speak.

"We're proud of all our seniors at Cornelia High," (one or two in the back ducked their heads) "and we wish you well as you go out into the world. For some of our students, this is a particularly rewarding time. But I hope for all of you it is a time of fulfillment." ("When is he going to stop stammering around?" whispered Stella beside Juliana.) "I know you're all anxious to hear who the two students are." (Everyone leaned forward in breathless expectancy.) "The reason it's taken so long is that our two top students are only a fraction of a point apart in their scores, and we wanted to be quite positive we had it right." He folded and refolded the paper. "According to the scores as they stand, I pronounce the valedictorian of the class of 1922—Miss Juliana Hamilton!"

The room exploded into cheers, but the principal held up a hand to quiet them. "There is more," he said. "We have a fine young man—(did he emphasize the word man?)—Spike Henderson is salutatorian." Cheers again, particularly from the male students. Then everyone fell silent and the whole room barely breathed, waiting for the final announcement.

The principal cleared his throat and wiped his face again. "This year our faculty has had the added responsibility of choosing, not only the top student, but the student with the highest average along with the most practical ambitions for using his or her talents. It is with pleasure that I offer the Walter K. Durden Scholarship to Spike Henderson!"

Sister was ecstatic on the way home. "You really are valedictorian. So what if you lost the scholarship? You really didn't want it, anyway. Being valedictorian was your goal, and you've made it! Won't Mamma be surprised! I'm so glad I took extra pains with your white graduation dress. All Mamma's pretty lace will be seen by everyone, and you'll look just like a queen."

"Sister! Please hush! We should have *both* been valedictorian, you know. I was only a fraction of a point ahead of Spike. He probably knows more math than I do."

"But you were ahead, and it's only right you should have the honor. Just think—my own little sister, a winner! I sure am going to miss you next year," said Sister in a burst of affection.

"*You* miss *me?* You're the one who's leaving. Why, you'll be so busy up there in North Carolina making all those children toe a straight line, you won't have time to think about us. But I—I don't know what I'll be doing."

"Take the class I'm leaving at Cornelia Elementary, Juliana. You would be so good. And they said today they still hadn't gotten anyone."

"I don't know. I guess right now I'll concentrate on writing my speech."

The auditorium was packed on graduation night. There were banks of mountain laurel in the front, and, down the aisle, a profusion of rose petals strewn by little girls in frilly dresses.

The heat was smothery, and a flick-flick could be heard all over the auditorium as everyone fanned their programs to stir the humid air. Juliana was about to maul hers to shreds as she waited for her turn to speak. She didn't hear Spike's speech nor the principal's. Strangely, it was Henry she was thinking about. He was there tonight with his girl friend Martha.

Just a few months ago he had declared he would never marry, but then Martha had come along, and though no public plans had been made, they all knew what Henry had in mind. But that was not what was uppermost in *her* thoughts now. It was the fact that Henry should have had a chance to graduate as she was doing. He should not have had to stay home all these years running the farm while the rest of them went to school. Few people realized how much Henry minded not having an education—but she knew. She had heard him talking to Maude, to Black and Gray, and more recently to stubborn old John. He told them everything, and she had heard him when he didn't know she was anywhere near. Why should it be that someone always had to sacrifice that others might have blessings?

She looked down at her carefully written speech, smudged now on the edges from her sweaty hands. There was one thing for sure. She wanted this speech to make Henry proud, and she wanted him and the rest of the family, and all her teachers, to know that she didn't take this privilege for granted, that she knew sacrifices had been made. Oh, she wouldn't embarrass

Henry. But he would know what she meant. She had practiced this speech so many times by Lorna Doone Slide that she had memorized it, word for word. But all of a sudden her throat tightened, and she wasn't sure she'd even be able to read it, much less recite it from memory.

When the time came she walked to the platform and, as Mamma had advised, stopped to take a deep breath before she began. That was when she saw him. Way in the back, on the very back row in fact, a head taller than those around him, sat Foster Kirk. Even from that distance she could see his scowling smile, and her knees turned to jelly beneath her. She had not seen him since that terrible night last winter. The blood rushed to her face at the very thought of that awful night, and she averted her gaze from his compelling look to seek out the row where her own family sat: Mamma and Henry with his Martha; Byron, just barely home from college; Brother, Winnie, and little Margo; Richard and Frances, with wigglesome Jack in her lap; Sister, and Grange who had come up alone, leaving a neighbor with Molly who was sick in bed. She was steadied by the comfortable familiarity of their faces.

Finally, she found her voice and began to speak, carefully avoiding looking anywhere near the back row. She didn't know how she got through. She felt she was reading woodenly instead of speaking with animation as she'd wanted to do. All the fine quotations so diligently gathered, and the resounding challenges to her fellow students, seemed somehow inappropriate and lame. When she finished, she started to leave the platform as quickly as possible, her face burning, but the principal took hold of her arm and stayed her, signing for her to look at the audience. Tears stung her eyes as she saw that, not only was everyone clapping, but they were all standing. As she looked, a movement in the back caught her eye. It was Foster Kirk striding out the door.

The day after graduation a package came to Juliana —a very puzzling package. She studied it all the way back from the mailbox, turning it over and over, gently rattling it, reading and rereading the postmark and the return address. If it were from Foster Kirk, and the handwriting was most definitely his, and if it were mailed in Cocoa Beach, Florida which the postmark plainly indicated, then who was it that she'd seen at graduation? It couldn't have been Foster Kirk. He wouldn't have mailed a package and then come himself, would he?

She sat down on the porch and fingered the firm, neat knot of twine in the middle of the hand-sized package. If he were keeping his promise not to see her for three years, or until her eighteenth birthday, he would have had to mail the package, no matter where he was. She wouldn't be eighteen until August 10. But how did she know he wasn't married? Perhaps he had just happened to be on her road last winter. After all, he was a businessman and an artist. He could have any number of reasons for being on that road. And she really had no reason to think he had more than a casual interest in her now. When she accepted that, she knew that it couldn't matter if she opened the package. He was simply being courteous and kind toward an old acquaintance, that was all.

She had not told anyone about seeing Foster the night before. It seemed unnecessary to cause any more trouble. Grange had left that morning on the early train and, if he'd known his old friend was around, he'd never mentioned it.

As she played with the knot on the package, she looked down to see that the string was loosening; the brown wrapping paper coming undone at one end. Without stopping to think, she unwrapped the little box and opened it up.

She didn't think she had ever seen anything so beautiful, unless it was violets in the spring, as the dainty necklace of tiny lavender seashells on a fine string, done quite professionally with a jeweler's catch for fastening it on. At first she just looked at it, then gently she began to finger the rounded shape of each shell and to trace with a fingernail the thread-sized lines on the back of each one. When she lifted it out from its velvet cushion, she saw a note underneath: "Wishing you all that you hope for. Always, Foster."

She was trying to fasten the necklace around her neck when she heard a firm step behind her. The screen opened, and Brother cleared his throat as he stood over her.

"From Foster Kirk?" he asked with a hardness in his voice, reaching out as if he would jerk the necklace away from her.

"Yes," she said, her hand closing around it protectively.

He stood there looking down at her in such a way that she felt his impatience and exasperation, though she would not look into his eyes. When he walked around to ease himself into a chair beside her, he let out a sigh that was almost a groan.

"Juliana, I thought that was all behind us. It is unbelievable that the man is still trying to contact you."

"Why? Couldn't love be that strong?"

"Of course. Yes. But for such a child?"

"I'm almost eighteen. I'm graduated, remember?"

"And he is twice as old as you, too! Marriage is a partnership—not a father-daughter relationship."

"He never seemed like a father to me."

"I suppose the war and hardship caused you to grow up quicker. But it didn't actually make you any older chronologically. If you were married to a man Foster's age, who would your friends be?"

"Brother, you can read this note. It doesn't sound serious. He is probably already married to—someone else. After all, we were friends, and it couldn't hurt for him to send me this small gift, could it? Look at the shells. Aren't they beautiful? I think he probably picked them up from the beach himself." She could imagine Foster Kirk bending his tall frame to pick up the pea-size shells, shells that would be lost in the big brown roughness of his hand.

There was a rattle of silver and dishes inside as Sister and Mamma put dinner on the table. Beside the porch steps a hummingbird hovered around a red lily. Far away a bobwhite called and after a minute another one answered from nearby, its call clear and distinct above the other little buzzing, sizzling sounds of summer.

"Juliana, I've been thinking. Mamma says you

really wanted that scholarship. You're a very good student, and it's quite a shame for you to stop now. I could tell from your speech that you've given a lot of serious thought to what God wants you to do with your life. There's an excellent college for girls in Red Springs, North Carolina, about an hour's train ride from Linden. If Henry and Richard can help some, we can send you to college."

"But—no!—it would cost too much!" she exclaimed.

"We can do it—somehow. Think about it." He rose and stretched as Sister called them to dinner.

At first she had wanted the scholarship so much and worked hard for it, was disappointed when she didn't get it, but then had really been relieved that she was to stay at home. Now here was Brother offering to send her to college when she knew very well there wasn't enough money.

The questions tumbled and turned in her head until Sister said one morning that sleeping with Juliana anymore was like sleeping with a rooting pig. She went to her favorite places, but even the waters of Lorna Doone Slide could not calm the churning inside her. How could she leave Clover Hill again? And what about Henry? If she left, that would mean he was the only one left to stay with Mamma. What would that do to his plans with Martha? And what if—just if—Foster Kirk wasn't married and he came back, and she wasn't even here?

One day as she walked toward the house from the orchard she heard voices in the barn as she came close, and dropped in to see what was going on.

"Who's here?" she called from the door.

"Me and the musk," said Henry's voice from back in a stall. "Don't come too close. I'm cleaning up."

She climbed the boards of a half-wall and perched there watching him wield the big shovel, filling a wooden wheelbarrow with horse droppings.

"So—Mamma says you might be going off again."

"Might."

"Good idea. A smart girl like you shouldn't be stuck in Habersham County, feeding chickens and weaning little calves."

"Habersham County's the best place in the whole world," she said.

"Think so? Can't tell until you try the rest of the world."

"*I* can."

"Oh, I see. Extra powers of perception. Well, I always knew you were made of special stuff. I guess that proves it."

"Henry . . ."

He stopped and leaned on the handle of the shovel, pulling out a dingy rag to mop the sweat out of his eyes. Then he looked up at her expectantly.

"Do you want me to go?" she asked.

He came to her, reached up and ran a rough, grimy finger down the curve of her cheek. "In a manner of speaking, no. I'll miss you like the dickens. Realistically, yes. What have I worked for all these years—to see you graduate from high school and then be like anybody else?"

"But, Henry, what about you? I know the apples

didn't sell all that well last year, and—well, Brother said . . ."

He shuffled his feet and thumped the big blade of the shovel against the floor several times, chopping up wads of dry dung. "The thing about me is—don't worry an inch or a pinch, either. I'm doing quite well for myself. Couldn't be better, in fact. There are always ways of managing, and I can't think of anything better to invest in than you."

"What about—you and Martha?" she asked, prying a splinter up on a rough board with her fingernail.

"Now you're getting into personal business, gal, which I'm not ready to relate. Just don't worry about me. Make your decision independent of me completely. Now you better run. You're keeping me from my work."

As she walked out she heard him resume his cheery whistle, and the rhythmic click, slide, thump of the shovel began again.

CHAPTER 13

IT WAS A SUNDAY in July. The heat assaulted them from every direction—from the dusty road, from the high clay road banks, from the quiet trees that looked deceptively cool in their sylvan setting. Even the wind was hot on their cheeks as the Hamiltons rode home from church. Juliana fanned herself with a Sunday school book with one hand and held onto her parasol with the other. She was very conscious of the shell necklace around her throat, the lavender strand just dipping down over the neckline of her white dress. Mamma had finally said she could keep it, and had let her write a thank-you note to Foster, though Brother had frowned on it and Henry had grunted that it was a good thing she was going off to school.

"I do feel in my bones that something is wrong at Clover Hill," said Mamma as they jogged along.

"Now, Mamma, you've said that three times.

You'll *make* something happen if you keep it up,'' said Sister.

''Watch this,'' said Henry. ''Watch Black cross this bridge. See? He never fails to step over that board we put in to replace the one he broke years ago. He can't tell by the newness which is which, because they're all weathered the same now. He's one smart horse.''

''I think Henry's going to be a bachelor and spend his days communing with his horses and listening to them eat,'' said Byron.

''Didn't you see him sitting to one side with Martha at the watermelon cutting last night?'' asked Sister.

''Oh, yes, but I remember also that he's never going to marry, because warring wives are a curse on any house.''

Henry clucked to the horses and said nothing.

''I do believe something is definitely wrong at home,'' said Mamma, as if she hadn't heard any of the other conversation.

''Now, Mamma,'' began Byron, as they came around the bend in sight of the Clover Hill road. ''But, wait,'' he said then, leaning forward in the surrey, ''whose cows are those in the road?''

''I knew it!'' said Mamma. ''Our cows are out. And don't they always get out on Sunday?''

They changed into old clothes, sniffed at the tantalizing smells coming from the kitchen, and reluctantly went to round up the cows, leaving Mamma to finish up the dinner. It was two hours later, even with the help of Blake and his brothers, before they got the livestock all back in the pasture.

''It's too hot to pack them in the barn,'' said Henry,

scratching his head. "They'll smother each other. You girls are going to have to watch them and keep them together while Byron and I check the fence and get it mended."

The boys disappeared and all was stickily still. The cows shifted uneasily, grazing and mooing by turns. Finally they grouped themselves under a wide spreading oak not far from the barn.

"I'll go bring us a drink of water," volunteered Juliana, and Sister quickly agreed.

Juliana's legs stung from briar scratches, and she was so hot that her face felt as if it were on fire. She saw that she had ripped the hem of her calico dress on one side and that she was covered with stick-tights. She walked up the steps, already relishing the feel of the cool well water going down her throat, when she heard a motor slow at their mailbox. It must be someone coming to see Martha and her family who lived in Grandmother's house, but just in case, she stepped quickly inside the door.

"Juliana, is that you?" called Mamma from the front room. Then, in consternation, "Juliana! We've got company. Oh, dear, I was so tired I've lain down here because it seemed like the coolest place. I don't even have my dress on. You do something with them till I get ready."

Juliana glanced again at her dress, hastily picked some stick-tights off, and tried to turn the hem back up where it would stay just for a few minutes. Maybe it was the minister. He had seen her already in all kinds of garb, even once in peach-peeling clothes. But when she peered out a window, she gasped in dismay. Foster Kirk was opening a car door for Miss Delia Sweet.

There was nothing to do but greet them graciously, standing at the top of the steps with her hands behind her back. At least they didn't have to see her dirty hands. She avoided looking into Foster Kirk's eyes.

"Let's sit here on the porch where it's not quite so hot," she invited. "Mamma will be out soon."

"I hope we didn't disturb an afternoon rest," said Miss Sweet, letting her eyes travel all the way from Juliana's moist face to her thick, clumsy shoes.

"How have you been?" asked Foster, not giving her time to respond to Miss Sweet's comment.

"We are all very well, thank you. How are Beppo and the cats?"

"Beppo is glad to be home again. He enjoyed the beach, but the weather is too hot for him there."

"Then are you back at Pinedale—to stay?"

"For a while, anyway."

"He'll probably send me packing down to Florida soon to keep an eye on that land while he settles in back here," said Miss Sweet, fanning herself with her own little folding fan decorated with pink roses. "He has this notion to have a house full of children some day and thinks he must invest heavily in land to pay for raising them. I do think he could have chosen some investment less clumsy to move around—like diamonds. But of course I quite like Florida. If it were up to me, he'd raise his family there in the clean salt spray."

Juliana was trying to think how she could tactfully ask whom Foster was marrying when she heard Sister shouting from below the barn. Her memory goaded her to action. Poor Sister down there thirsting in the hot sun all this time! She hurried into the kitchen and drew a jar of water, then ran back across the porch, turning toward the visitors from halfway down the steps to say in confusion, "Excuse me, please!"

She saw Foster's eyes twinkle in amusement. As she started quickly across the yard, she heard him talking low to Miss Sweet, probably making fun of her appearance and strange behavior. Just as she turned the corner of the house, she saw the cows ambling toward her, cropping along, eating Mamma's lilies, two of them heading back toward the garden. Sister had come in sight around the barn, with her dress tucked up for running, but let it fall suddenly when she saw Foster Kirk coming up beside Juliana.

"Here," said Juliana to Foster, without taking her eyes from the two cows. "Hold this water. I'll head them off this way, Sister. You keep them from running toward the field."

She tried to block them neatly. But in the manner of the willful beasts they are, they broke around her, bellowing and flicking their tails. Then, settling back into a determined gait, they headed straight for the garden, generous milk bags swinging.

Juliana circled around and had at last aimed them in the right direction, though they were making a meal off the bean vines at the same time, when there was a thunderous pounding of hooves to her left. She looked up to see six cows bolting from in front of the house with Foster right behind them, shouting and waving his arms, water sloshing from the jar still clutched in his hand.

Juliana could not imagine one not knowing that cows must not be run—guided, prodded, encircled, pushed, and shoved—but never run. Now they were all out of control, galloping wildly, trampling the garden mercilessly, even running into the woods toward the hog pen.

Juliana planted herself in front of Foster who was still waving the jar of water and shouting. "Foster Kirk!" she yelled, her hands on her hips. "We're trying to make the cows go toward the barn, not everywhere else. Take this whip and leave the jar of water. I'll teach you how to drive cows."

Thirty minutes later they had the cows herded back into the pasture just as Byron and Henry walked up, shaking their heads.

"We haven't found a single place they could have gotten out," Byron said.

"You went too far," said Sister. "Here—right next to the gate. Looks for all the world as if someone had cut the wires. I saw the cows come through, only it was the last ones I saw, not the first, unfortunately."

"Why weren't you watching as I told you to?" asked Henry, his brow heavily furrowed as he examined the wires.

"I thought they were safe, and I went to sleep. Juliana had gone to get us a drink of water."

Foster Kirk broke into laughter and they all turned to look at him in amazement. "So that was what the water was for!" he said. "I just couldn't imagine why you used water to chase cows!"

"And just what are *you* doing here?" demanded Henry, not cracking a smile.

"He's come to visit us all," said Juliana, stamping a small foot. "And you don't have to be rude about it."

"I think it's time we ate dinner," said Byron. "I starved several hours ago and now I feel as if I'm dying all over again. Come on, Henry, let's fix this hole while the girls put dinner on. Say, do you really think someone cut the wires?"

"It's quite obvious they did. Only thing is—who?"

"The Ku Klux Klan?" asked Sister.

"The Ku Klux Klan!" said Foster, stepping forward, every trace of laughter gone from his lean face. "If you really think . . . I've a job with the *Atlanta Constitution,* and they're trying to expose these sorry rascals and bring them to justice."

"We don't need help from Atlanta to manage our affairs," said Henry, his eyes blazing. "I don't know who cut the wires, but they've got to be fixed, and then—well, I suppose since you're here, you might as well eat with us."

Foster's face went pale and he gripped the top of the fencepost, then let his hand drop to his side. "I accept the invitation. And as to outside managing of your affairs, I couldn't agree with you more. That's why I'm a Republican. However, we're both in favor of the law being observed, I believe . . ."

"Juliana," said Sister, tugging at her arm. "Let's put dinner on."

To Juliana's relief, the three men were chatting amiably as they walked up the porch steps a short time later. Apparently no one was worrying any more about who cut the fence, and she kept her own ideas to herself. Poor Blake had gotten into quite enough trouble already.

The conversation around the table was lively. Juliana, who had quickly cleaned up and slipped back into her white dress with the strand of shells at her throat, found it quite fascinating to watch Foster Kirk's face as it changed from a scowl of concentration to a relaxed laugh, his dark eyes lighting with interest as he conversed. Whenever he looked her way, she dropped her eyes quickly, and hoped no one noticed that her heart seemed to beat up in her throat, making the shells pulsate. Why had she never noticed before that he had an intriguing space between his front teeth?

After dinner the men went out to look at Foster's car. It was his own, it seemed, an Essex he'd driven back from Cocoa Beach. It had all the newest features—doors that opened toward the front instead of suicide doors, an automatic starter, and, according to Foster, it was a champion for climbing hills, sturdy with a lot of pick-up. What Juliana saw was a smart black carriage with see-through window curtains. She wondered if Maureen had already had a ride in it.

"Miss Sweet, did you take all those cats to Florida?" Sister was asking.

"Oh, yes, and brought back more than I took. It was a bit of a hard trip, though. To be as messy as he is around the house, Foster is religiously particular about that car. You would think that someone who never thinks to throw away his apple cores could tolerate a few well-mannered cats in his car. He says he won't take them back again so, if I go, I'll have to get someone to care for them."

"Cutting up the mice and all?"

"Certainly. Only the Lord can help the person who mistreats one of my cats."

"That sounds rather severe," said Mamma.

"Perhaps so, but people can take care of themselves, while the little creatures are dependent on us."

"I can't help feeling sorry for the poor little mice," murmured Juliana.

Miss Sweet turned sharply toward her. "Don't you know that mice were created for the consumption of cats, child?" Juliana could see Foster walking toward them, but Miss Sweet's back was to him, and she kept talking. "Foster has this odd notion of marrying. Well, I've already told him it must be understood that my cats were in the family first, and if his *wife,*" here she bent a significant glare on Juliana, "if his *wife* doesn't like them, it's just too bad."

"Yes, and I tell her priorities are not always formed that simply." Miss Sweet gave a slight start at the sound of Foster's deep voice right at her elbow, and looked up to see his jaw set firmly. "I'm not a man of fancy speeches, nor did I intend to make my mission here a secret to you. I didn't mean to be so abrupt, either. But now that my aunt has brought the subject up for the second time today, I think I had better explain. I have come seeking Juliana as my wife."

It seemed as if the whole house gasped. Juliana longed to fade into the woodwork as she saw the storms gathering on her brothers' faces, saw them take threatening steps toward Foster. But Foster raised his hand firmly and continued to talk.

"I know she will not be eighteen until August 10, but surely you can allow me to start calling these few short weeks ahead of time. If it had not been for the glimpse of her on her graduation night, I would never have been able to wait this long, I'm afraid. If you only knew how hard these three years have been. Aunt De does, to an extent, and can verify that I've worked hard, clearing Florida wilderness land on Cape Canaveral, accumulating investments for taking care of a wife and raising a family."

Miss Sweet grunted disapprovingly.

Henry faced him squarely now, his fists clenching and unclenching at his sides. "We don't doubt your ability to take care of her. To be plain, Mr. Kirk, you're just not right for her. You're in the wrong generation. My sister has other plans that do not include you. I must ask you now, knowing your intentions, to leave."

There was a gasp from Miss Sweet who attempted to rise from her chair.

"Not so fast," said Mamma, coming to stand between the two men who were glaring at each other as if a fist fight might erupt at any moment. They stuffed their hands in their pockets as Mamma turned to Foster. "Juliana has decided to go to college at Flora McDonald in Red Springs, North Carolina." Juliana swallowed hard as she saw Foster, even with his deep Florida tan, turn pale. "She will be leaving in September and will be gone until June. She wants to continue her education, and I think, surely, you wouldn't want to interfere, being an educated man yourself. However, we did promise that you could call on Juliana after three years, and you have kept your end of the promise—almost, anyway—and we'll keep ours, provided . . ." She stepped back at that point and looked firmly at Juliana. ". . . provided it's all right with Juliana. That means you could visit her until she leaves, and if she changes her mind and decides to marry, then we'll have to go along with it."

"Mamma! No! Juliana *cannot* change her mind!" exploded Henry, pounding one fist into the other hand.

"Henry, when a girl is eighteen she has certain rights. I might say I don't think she will change her mind, but Foster can try within reasonable limits. So it's up to Juliana."

Everyone was quiet, waiting to hear from Juliana —so quiet that all she could hear was the shallow panting of Spring lying at her feet. Everyone was waiting for her to speak. It was far worse than making the speech at graduation, and what she wanted to do more than anything was to run.

"Juliana?" prodded Foster Kirk gently.

"But—Maureen," she stammered.

"Maureen who?"

"I—I mean I thought you were going to marry her."

"Marry Maureen? I have never once thought of marrying anyone else since first I saw you that Sunday afternoon."

"Oh," she said, and fidgeted with the shells at her neck.

"That was where we went wrong," grumbled

Henry just under his breath, "letting those kids go gallivanting on a Sunday."

"If you ask me," said Miss Sweet, "and, of course nobody did or we wouldn't even be here, but it seems to me if the child is going to wear the necklace we made, then she could at least accept a few well-intended calls."

Foster glowered at his aunt and went to Juliana, dropping on one knee beside her.

"Juliana, I don't want you to do anything you don't want to do. All I'm asking is a chance. If I can't make you return my love—then I won't pester you anymore. But I do warn you, I don't give up easily. May I visit you for the rest of the summer?" His eyes were demanding, his big, brown hand on the arm of her chair flexing nervously.

"Yes," she said quietly. "But I am going to college. No one is going to change my mind about that."

CHAPTER 14

FOSTER CAME TWICE a week, and sometimes more often. At first he only stayed for an hour or two, and the visit was very proper, with Juliana seating him in the front room and serving him his favorite drink—cool buttermilk. But as time went by Foster persuaded Mamma to let them go on walks together—to the falls, to Indian Hill, or all the way back past Ghost Den Ridge to Cold Spring. He listened, enchanted, as Juliana told him stories of the Ridge, and he could be as quiet as she when they knelt to peer by turns into the cavelike nest of a Carolina wren. Mamma said Foster must have been homesick for family living for years the way he so jubilantly took part in even their simplest forms of entertainment—listening to records or playing dominoes.

Henry, who himself was visiting Martha often these days, seemed to have softened toward Foster and enjoyed talking to him.

"He is a person of overwhelming honesty," he said. "And he knows a lot about land, just not much about farming." He grinned at the memory of Sister's description of Foster's cattle-driving ability.

Byron was not happy about his sister's being with Foster so much. But since he was sure that once she got off to college she would be attracted to someone her own age, he made no serious attempts to discourage her. No one knew just what Sister was thinking about the situation. The most she would say was, "Let her make up her own mind. It's her decision."

Once when Grange and Molly were visiting, they took Juliana and Mamma to see Foster Kirk at Pinedale. It certainly was not Grange's idea. It was the last place he wanted to take Juliana, and he said so. He told Mamma over and over that she needed to put a stop to this romance, that it had gone quite far enough. But Mamma only answered with such comments as, "She could do worse, you know," or "Age isn't everything, Grange."

When Grange offered to take them riding and Juliana suggested they go to Pinedale, Grange came close to exploding. "Do you really think I'm going to take you right into the lion's den?" he asked.

"He is kind of like a lion, isn't he?" said Juliana with a smile and a toss of her hair.

"Don't be saucy with me, young lady! You know what I'm talking about."

"Yes, I know. You introduced me to Foster yourself. He was one of your best friends, and now you're not being very loyal."

"I would never have introduced you if I'd known it

would come to this. He *was* my best friend, but you were my friend first. Now, listen, Juliana, be reasonable . . ."

"Don't ask a woman to be reasonable, Grange," said Molly, fanning herself slowly. "Go ahead and take her. Don't you know that denying her will make her run right to him?"

"It will not make any difference either way!" said Juliana, her cheeks very pink. "You can do whatever you want to do. It will not make any difference."

It was odd—approaching Pinedale by the road instead of walking in from the train. The little gray houses looked the same as before, though, with maybe a little more ivy creeping up the porch pillars of the cottage.

As they walked up the narrow path, Juliana looked from side to side taking in all the dear, familiar sights and smells. Foster had been telling her that he regularly got up at four in the morning to work outside and only went back to the house to paint after the sun was up. She could see now the results of his labors. Foster had planted mountain hemlocks near the turn-around and an ivy bush by the path near the studio. Foster called it a laurel, but she had always known it as ivy. The lawn was neatly trimmed, but the woods crowded in around the edges. Even so, she could see at a glance that work had been going on, for there was a fallen tree cut into lengths, and out toward the moss-grown graves of Foster's mother and grandmother, the path had been carefully trimmed.

They were almost to the cottage steps before Beppo suddenly discovered them, dashing toward them, his teeth bared. Molly screamed and hid behind Grange, but Juliana held out her hand and said, "Quiet, boy," whereupon there was a creak of the studio floor, and Foster emerged, a look of astonished pleasure on his rugged face.

Foster was dressed in khakis that looked as if they might have just barely survived the war, and his face and neck were blackened with a healthy stubble of beard. But he spent no time in apologizing for his appearance.

"Aunt De is visiting the neighbors," he explained as he seated them. "She's teaching someone to sew, I think. So—tell me, Grange, how are things in the big city? At the church? And have you seen the Colvins lately?"

"Just a minute now. You're shooting questions too fast to answer. If you're so interested, why don't you come back down and join us?"

"Unfortunately I am going to have to come down this fall for a short time. I have an exhibit scheduled in October. But I won't be gone a minute longer than I have to."

"I can see why you wouldn't want to leave," said Mamma. "This is such a peaceful, beautiful place."

"I'm glad you like it—and—well, let me get you all some cool grape juice. I picked the grapes this morning from the vine there at the edge of the lawn, and Aunt De squeezed them and put the juice in the spring. Walk with me, Juliana?"

The pathway was shaded nearly all the way by oaks and hemlock and sweetgum. Thick carpets of myrtle and fern stretched beneath the trees, and along the path bloomed Indian pinks and brown-eyed Susans. They paused at the top of the damp, mossy stone steps which led down to the rock-walled spring. Juliana played self-consciously with a glossy leaf of a large rhododendron bush, tracing the heavy veins on the pale underside.

"It is precious to me that you've come, little one. It's been a long, long time since you were here." Foster's hands were behind his back where he could keep them in control.

"I know. I wanted very much to see it again, so when Grange offered to take us riding, I asked to come here."

"You like it here then?" he asked eagerly, taking a step nearer.

"Oh, very much. Wouldn't anyone?" she asked, lifting wondering blue eyes.

"Not everyone. Some would, in the name of progress, cover every available space with cities and towns, ignoring the need for nature's cycles, the need for standing trees, tiny mosses and lichens, little mushrooms, squirrels, birds. By the way," he said, setting one foot on a large stone and leaning forward on his knee, "I'd like to show you the brooks and streams here at Pinedale. Some haven't been named yet, and I'd like to see what you would name them. You have a wonderful imagination."

"What makes you think so?"

His heart raced at the flash of sudden delight in her eyes.

"Do you think I didn't even listen to your graduation speech or that I haven't noticed your charming observations about the world around you? Besides wanting you to name the streams, I'd just like you to see them, because—well, because I know you love to watch flowing water."

"Oh, yes, I do! And—Foster, your place is so beautifully—well, natural. I do hope it will never be spoiled." She looked up into lofty treetops as she spoke.

"It won't be if I have anything to do with it. I'll admit—it's partly selfishness on my part. I love it as it is—untouched, pure—so I don't want it changed and will fight to keep it this way. But it's more than that. Years from now people many miles from here will benefit from this bit of forestland, absorbing the rains and holding them, providing oxygen. And it will be a place where man can view nature as God created it—without a clutter of concrete. And—there could be many children who would call this place home and love it as you love your Clover Hill."

She listened with great concentration as he talked. But when he mentioned children, her eyelids fell. "What painting are you working on now?" she asked quickly, to cover her embarrassment.

"I'm doing one called 'Woodlands.' For some reason I'm having trouble concentrating, though. I think you know why. By the way, though the picture I did of you wasn't very good, do you suppose I could borrow it back for a while? So many times I've wished I had begged to keep it, poor as it was, if it was all I could have of you."

"Mamma might let you borrow it back. It belongs to her, but if you talk just right, she'd let you have it

. . . and now don't you think we'd better get the grape juice?"

"Oh, Juliana . . . always the one for finishing conversations neatly, closing things up."

A shadow fell across her face. "Did I say something wrong?"

"Not at all. It's just always time to go, it seems. We only get started talking, and it's time to go." He reached out and lifted her chin with one finger. "But don't worry. I never want you to have to worry, little one," he said, and came so close she was sure he was going to kiss her. His eyes were full of tenderness, and her whole body seemed to be reaching out to him, though she was standing very still. Suddenly he dropped his hand and walked quickly down the steps where she heard a slosh and pattering drip as he plucked a glass jar from the cool water and started back with it.

When Foster and Juliana got back to the cottage porch, they found the rest of the group sitting very quietly watching a house wren feeding her young in a nest at the top of a pillar.

"The little bird doesn't mind our being here at all apparently," said Mamma, accepting a glass of grape juice from Foster.

"No. I think after learning to live with all Aunt De's cats, the birds are quite fearless—to a point, anyway." He placed the glass jug on the low wall and then sat down on the wall himself near Juliana's chair. "That's a favorite home for the little wrens. I'd like to think it's the very same couple that lived there last year and the year before. But without marking their wings, I can't tell for sure."

"They're such cute little brown birds," said Juliana softly.

Mamma laughed gently. "Juliana has always been completely fascinated by little things."

"Especially little things that were models of big things," said Grange. "Remember the set of tiny furniture Byron made you? Do you still have it?"

Juliana shook her head. "I gave it to Margo."

"This is good juice, Foster," said Molly, finding an opening in the conversation. "It's almost as cool as if it had been in our refrigerator."

"Your refrigerator?" inquired Mamma in surprise. "Why, you two didn't tell us you'd gotten yourselves a refrigerator."

"We just did," said Grange. "Two weeks ago. It's the newest on the market."

"I hope you don't die of asphyxiation from the carbon dioxide," said Foster, standing to refill the empty glasses.

"No, no, Foster, they've discovered a new coolant now. Call it Freon. It's quite safe."

"And so much more pleasant than having to buy big blocks of ice all the time," said Molly, rocking herself gently in the swing.

"Well, you must be doing quite well for yourself, old chap," said Foster. "Your job's agreeing with you and your pocketbook."

"Not bad, if I do say so," said Grange with a grin. Juliana thought to herself that Grange seemed to have forgotten his animosity toward Foster, and she was glad.

All too soon the afternoon shadows lengthened, and

it was time to go. Foster walked with them down to the car. At one point he managed a walk with Mamma a little apart from the others and, bending his head so as to speak quietly, he asked her if he might borrow the painting of Juliana. She had been holding to his arm as he helped her down a difficult step, and now she stopped, looking up at him with widened eyes.

"If it's all right with Juliana," she said finally.

He nodded. "She said to speak to you about it and you might let me have it if I asked just right. I'm afraid at times I'm lacking sorely in the social graces. I want the picture and so I'm asking for it straight out."

"You may certainly borrow it then. I appreciate your honesty more than you can know."

Foster came to Juliana's eighteenth birthday dinner. He brought her a novel, *Ivanhoe,* by Sir Walter Scott. On the flyleaf he had written: "No matter how things turn out, I will always love you."

She considered that sentiment as she sat with her back to a tree one day. Did she love him or was it just *his* love drawing her to him? And, now that she thought about it, did he love her or was she just a part of his big dream of preserving nature and raising a big family? Because if he didn't love her for herself, there was no sense in continuing to think about him. These were things she had to know.

She told him shyly one day about her desire to help someone, to do something special. She was grateful to him for listening with such interest, but in the end she knew he didn't really understand.

"Wouldn't a dozen of your own children be mission

field enough for you?" he asked quite seriously.

"A dozen?"

"Well, give or take a few."

"Foster Kirk, you are too ambitious!" she declared.

They talked about poetry, art, kittens, and kings. She showed him the field, "Judy's Little Acre," where one year she'd grown sixty bushels of corn, becoming the champion grower of the Boys' Corn Club. Sometimes he brought his sketch pad, and they sat beside a large tree or by Lorna Doone Slide, talking about colors—how the light and shadow changed the shades of blue and green—about the shapes of the forest, the pillars of pine, and the circular sun patterns falling through the chaos of windblown leaves.

"The Lord has given examples all around us of the impossible made possible, of confusion changed to order, and of beauty from ugliness," he said one day. "Take that old rotten log there with ferns and moss taking it over. It's a perfect example of something stark and black becoming, not just covered by, but part of something beautiful."

Juliana had been watching Foster as he spoke, his hands gesturing expressively. "And so death becomes life," she breathed softly, and answered his gaze steadily when he turned.

Foster tried to persuade her to go to school in Atlanta, if she must go to school somewhere. That way he could at least see her. But she would never even consider it.

"Juliana, you are so stubborn!" he said one day at summer's end, standing up and walking the floor, his hands fisted in his pockets. "Why must you be so stubborn? If only I could make you see that learning can go on without college, that you could have all the books you wanted. College sterilizes a person. You'll be educated all right, just the way the professors want you—every student coming off the graduation line like peas out of a pod, all just alike."

"You lay little value to individuality in that case," said Juliana, sparks flying as she rose to face him. "If I'm different in the first place, won't I react differently? Don't you think I have any control over myself? Isn't it really that you think I'm not deeply intelligent enough for further education? Isn't that really the issue?"

"How can you say that? I've told you over and over . . ." He paused in front of a window, his back to her, and took several deep breaths before he turned around. Then he began again, "It's your spontaneity, your spark, your wonderful positive attitude of anticipating what may happen next. I'm afraid you'll lose that in institutional learning."

She laid a hand on his arm. "Foster, I have to go. Maybe when I come back, I'll be the wife you need."

"You're the wife I need right now."

"No, I'm not. Because, you see, I don't know whether I love you or not." She was looking him right in the eyes as she spoke, and she saw him flinch as if she'd stabbed him. Then his shoulders sagged.

"When are you leaving?" he sighed.

"Tomorrow."

"Then I won't see you again?"

"Not for a while."

He picked up his hat, turned to look at her one more time, then walked out. She stood leaning against the side of the door, watching him go and aching with longing to love him the way he wanted her to.

Henry took Juliana and Byron to meet the train in Cornelia. Mamma had not gone to see Sister off the week before and chose to tell the two youngest good-by at home, also. "It's easier that way," she said brightly, adjusting a bow on Juliana's dress as if she were a small girl again.

"Now, Mamma, don't you cry or I'll start," said Juliana, stamping a foot on the porch floor where they stood waiting for Henry to bring the buggy around.

"I'll try, honey. But, you see, you're my last one. And—I guess I'm afraid you'll never be my same little Juliana again."

"I haven't been your *little* Juliana for a long time, Mamma. But I'll always be your big Juliana, who loves you very much. Now write often. Here's Henry—"

Foster, as well as Mamma, feared the changes that might come to Juliana in the months she was away. Would she grow away from him completely and learn to love someone else? The night before she was to leave, he walked the floor of his little studio, unable to sleep.

"Should I give up? Can I give up?" he moaned aloud as he stood at the window where he could look up to the dark tossing of treetops against the lighter sky. Those trees grew above the grave of his mother whose companionship he had missed so much all these years. There had never been anyone to take her place. And if he lost Juliana, there would never be anyone to fill her place, either. The lonesomeness would be even worse now that he had known what it was like to be near her, to commune with her on subjects of the soul, mind, and heart. And, yes, she would never be the same again. She was leaving, and the true Juliana—the one who had become as much a part of him as his own breath—might never return.

As soon as the first dawn light showed, Foster took his axe and went to the woods where he began cutting small deformed striplings, laying them in a central pile for chopping into firewood. The chips flew, and time after time he heaved good-sized poles onto his shoulders, almost relishing in the harsh rubbing weight of the wood.

When it was light enough he went in, washed his face, and tried to paint. But he felt as if he were fighting with the canvas, as if the symmetry of nature had turned to hard angles, as if colors actually were flat and there was no sunshine in the green of summer trees or the blue of distant mountains—or the memory of golden hair and gentian eyes that said so much, yet kept a secret always. Finally he threw down a piece of chalk, looked at his watch, and walked briskly to his car. Aunt De called after him, wanting to know where he was going, but all he said was that he would be back.

Juliana was having a very hard time keeping the tears back as she and Byron waited on the platform, their suitcases by their feet. She had thought it wouldn't be so bad since she was going to make the trip with Byron. But she had told Mamma good-by—and Clover Hill—and now it was almost time to tell Henry good-by. She couldn't help wondering why she had gotten herself into this. Hadn't she said once—many times—that she would never leave Clover Hill? And yet she was doing so of her own free will. Of course Brother and the rest of the family had encouraged her, but no one had said she had to go. It was her own decision, just as she had reminded Foster very heatedly one day when he accused her of doing whatever her brothers told her to.

"I hear it coming," said Henry. "I'll help you get on, Judy. Now, girl, don't break my neck. Save the pieces, will you? Come on, let's go."

She found a seat where she could watch Henry as they pulled away from the station. She was able to smile through her tears at the comical way in which he stood, impatient to leave, scratching crosses in the dust with his boot toe, yet looking up often to see if she were still there.

"He's going to be feeling much better when he gets us out of his way," said Byron.

"Byron! Look!" said Juliana, pointing beyond Henry to a black Essex that came to a jerking halt almost at the same instant a tall figure leapt from it. "Foster," she breathed. "Byron, let me by, I must go tell him good-by."

"You can't! The train's pulling out! There, don't you feel it? Just wave. It's all you can do."

Foster had started running, but stopped as he saw

the train moving. Now he stood beside Henry, his hat off, waving to the spot Henry said was Juliana's window—though all he could see was a blur of white.

CHAPTER 15

Pinedale
September 12, 1922

Dear Juliana,

I know I have been impatient with you, but it's only because you're the dearest one in the world to me. Now I'm hoping that you will forgive me for my harshness on my last visit, and let me begin again with a fresh slate. If I can't be everything to you right now, let me be what I can be. I once thought it was very unmanly to agree to be only friends with the one you loved, but that was before I knew what it was to love.

Your Mamma sends love to you, too, though by now you will have her own letter, for I mailed it myself. I went to your house to see if I could learn anything about you. She had not heard from you herself, so we comforted each other.

I had not realized how keenly lonesome it would make me to go to your house, and find no dear girl in blue tissue gingham smiling at me, teasing me into a laugh.

Your Mamma invited me into the front room, but seeing my downcast spirits, allowed me to talk with her in the dining room. It was just that I was going to miss you so much more in that room where we have spent so many hours listening to records and talking.

It is dawn now. Just light enough for me to see to write. It is the moment before even the pinkness shows through the screen of trees to the east, the moment when the birds go crazy with enthusiasm for whatever is to come (like another Little Bird I know), the moment when the light that is almost not light reflects off of night and brings form and color to what was only hunks and slabs of varying blackness.

Dear Girl, please write to me—write about anything you wish. And if you should at some time begin to have some deep feelings for me, let me know quickly. Now it is time for me to pull the weeds out of the myrtle bed before I start painting. Don't study too hard.

Always,
F.K.

"Juliana Hamilton!" The sharp voice jarred her from the peaceful world of Pinedale and the thought of Foster Kirk's dark head bent in concentration—jarred her suddenly back to the confines of the dormitory at Flora McDonald College. "Are you going to stand there all day mooning over that letter? I'm sure someone is paying dearly for you to come to school, and you shouldn't be dawdling your time away."

There were several things about the college that Juliana had disliked on sight. Heading the list was the woman with the strident voice who had met her upon her arrival. Lucretia Morgan had introduced herself as the housemother in a way that seemed to indicate she had the authority of a judge and jury combined and would never be caught this side of death handing down mercy to anyone. Behind her back she was known as "The Morgue." She wore nothing but black, and found occasion to say something derogatory about the pretty dresses worn by the girls in her dormitory. Her heavy eyebrows appeared, whether they were or not, to be constantly drawn in condemnation. Her lips were thin and straight, and she smiled only when someone was in trouble.

Juliana soon found that, even if she rushed in from the library five minutes before the deadline, she would still be put on restriction. "The Morgue" always sat at her desk like a cat quietly waiting to pounce on its unsuspecting victim. Juliana was often that victim. As Miss Lucretia said, "Five more minutes, young lady, and you'd be put on restriction, so I'd better go ahead and give it to you so you won't forget."

Another bitter disappointment was the water. Not the drinking water, as bad as it tasted, but the streams, if you could call them streams. The water was so red it looked black from the iron content. There were no falls or rapids, no pleasant gurgles around stones. The water just sat there, and only if you studied it for minutes at a time could you see any flow, even if you threw in a leaf to measure it. This was most distressing to Juliana who loved the movement, the rushing, the forever seeking of the Clover Hill creeks and the Chattahoochee River.

But the main problem with the water was that it spoiled the girls' clothes in the laundry. Juliana's pretty white dress, trimmed with Mamma's finely made lace, was no longer really white. And her blue gingham, Foster's favorite, looked dingy in between the blue. It was no wonder, she told her roommate, that The Morgue wore only black. It was the only color that would come through the wash the same as it went in.

But some things more than compensated for the annoyances. One was her French teacher, who was very demanding but fair. Juliana found a challenge in the "no English" limitation, in writing original essays in French, in translating a French newspaper. Miss Gerard began calling her aside after class to have conversations in French, commenting that very few of her second-year students took such an interest.

"You have had very good language instructors," she said.

"Yes, my brother taught me Latin for one year," said Juliana proudly, "and then my favorite teacher in Cornelia, Miss Shannon, taught Latin and French."

"We will work hard," insisted Miss Gerard. "You have much talent. It must not be wasted."

Juliana said little about her French class in her letters to Foster. She couldn't seem to write about it without sounding as though she were bragging, and, besides, she wasn't sure he would like it at all. He still didn't understand her burning desire to learn all she could, even though he himself was an avid learner.

Instead, she wrote to him about the silent movies, the lyceums, the art exhibits, the Highland fling, which was the one dance pronounced acceptable for students at this Scottish school. She wanted to be very honest with Foster, so every time Byron came over from Chapel Hill and brought a friend to escort her to the movie or concert, she told him about it. She didn't mention how boring the friends were.

Juliana was often the first to look for mail in the tiny room of pigeonholes behind The Morgue's desk. She realized one day that it wasn't a letter from Mamma she was most eager to find, but one bearing Foster Kirk's impossible scrawl. As she read, her cheeks would glow a soft pink. She hoped that only her roommate noticed, and not Lucretia Morgan!

She devoured Foster's description of Pinedale in autumn, and of Clover Hill where he visited often. Also, she enjoyed his character sketches of people whom he met while selling Essex cars in a new part-time business. Sometimes his letters bore a Florida postmark. He would tell about meeting a python at late dusk on his way through the scrub, or of killing a six-foot rattlesnake on the beach below his house.

"This is rough country," he wrote once. "Today we needed supplies, but it had rained so much it was necessary for me to walk into the village to get them. The Essex, as tough as it is, couldn't be expected to travel through that boggy sand. But I enjoyed the walk. The sunsets here make me ache to get them all on paper. Not one is the same as another. And, though I miss the hills of Habersham, there is a certain beauty in the swamp grass, the egrets, and the powerful, majestic, forever-rolling ocean."

"Please get your rest," he urged in another letter. "I love you so dearly that I simply cannot help worrying about you up there toiling over your books. I am living in the hope that you will decide one year of this is enough.''

''What about *your* rest?'' she responded. ''You talk casually about getting up at 4:00 A.M. and working until dark, then reading and writing into the night. Since your last letter when you told me about the mushrooms you cooked up for breakfast, I've been wondering if I was going to hear of your having poisoned yourself.''

Mamma enclosed a clipping from the *Constitution* of one of Foster's poems. ''Far blue hills, apple hills, red clay hills of Georgia,'' she read and could see with a pang of homesickness not only the hills but the author, dark eyes intent, hands behind back, looking out from his hilltop to the twin slopes of Trey or the craggy-sided Yonah.

She had a cry in her tiny room when she learned that Henry and Martha had married and were living at Clover Hill with Mamma. How sad, she thought, that out of their big family only Richard and Mamma were there for Henry's wedding. She didn't like to think of how different Clover Hill must be now with a new mistress and no one going to school on cold mornings, or coming home to raid the warming closet of leftover baked potatoes and biscuits.

It was Mamma who told Juliana that Henry had sold John and that they were using either Black or Gray for the buggy now. The reason Henry gave was that John was too stubborn for the womenfolk to handle, but Juliana remembered how he'd said, ''There's always a way to manage.'' She suspected he'd sold the horse and given up his own house plans so she could go to school. Lucretia Morgan was right. Someone *was* paying dearly for her to come to school, and she vowed anew that it would not be in vain. She would make sure she made good use of this year and learned every bit that she could.

Juliana had the growing feeling that she was being watched closely at mail time. The Morgue's eyes seemed always to follow her every move, and once Juliana caught her holding a letter up to the window and peering at it intently, as if trying to read the signature through the thin envelope. Juliana impulsively snatched it from her, and was promptly put on a week's restriction. Not being allowed to go to the library meant she made a "D" on a research paper that was due.

She asked Foster never to send her any postcards, as she didn't want The Morgue to read them. She did not tell him about the time she was sitting in the parlor studying French when a young man kissed his girl, and The Morgue put every girl in the parlor on restriction. Even after the girl explained that her beau had just asked her to marry him and she had accepted, The Morgue smiled with her tight lips and pointed to the stairs.

One day she had a letter from Miss Delia Sweet. She thought it rather odd, but nice. She had wondered how she would ever live with Aunt De if she did marry Foster. It was encouraging to have a friendly letter from her, though she was disturbed to learn that Foster was doing very little painting now that his exhibit was over. He was working hard in the woods and selling only a few cars.

"Today," wrote Foster, "I am making pencil drawings of the English-style stone house I plan to build on Hilltop. I'm planning to use a lot of gables and arches. The structure will be of flint and granite hauled down from the mountains. Our Creator made flint stone in varying muted colors that change with the changing lights. Beautiful! I have my eye on a little used truck that will be just the thing for hauling. If only my lady love would say yes to me, and would help me plan this house. . ."

Why is it so frightening to think of planning a house? Juliana asked herself as she looked out at the flat, rain-bedraggled campus of Flora McDonald. *Or of planning a family? Having babies? I do want babies—just like Margo, and Baby Jack, and Peter. But—a dozen? I'm just not old enough. There are other things I must do first.*

Autumn seemed interminable, despite the variety of interesting activities. The day Juliana got the news that Foster was bringing Mamma to Brother's where she, Byron, and Sister would meet for Christmas, she could have turned cartwheels if there had been a place where she could be sure The Morgue wouldn't see her from behind some curtain. As the days drew near, her dreams were constantly filled with what she would say to Foster, how he would look, whether or not he might kiss her. She set to work embroidering a tiny picture of a bright red cardinal to give him, taking care that her stitches were even neater than usual.

Because of her schedule, Juliana was the last to arrive in Linden for the Christmas gathering. Brother and Byron met her at the station, full of descriptions of the wonderful dinner being prepared. "The people in my church heard my family was coming," said Brother, "and they must have felt quite sorry for me. They have been arriving by twos and threes with dishes of this and that—cakes, pies, a turkey, loaves of bread, even some butter. You'll feel as if you're back home at Clover Hill, Juliana."

She wondered why Foster had not ridden with them, but would not ask. She knew it must have been because Brother didn't want him to.

She had barely gotten out of the car at the house when a small figure flung itself into Juliana's arms, almost knocking her over.

"Margo! Don't be so rough!" commanded Brother.

"Oh, it's all right," said Juliana happily. "Margo, how I've missed you! And haven't you grown! Next thing we know, you'll be starting to school."

"And can I go to school with you, Judy? Wouldn't that be fun!"

"Yes, wouldn't it!" Juliana hugged the little girl while she looked over her shoulder, expecting any minute to see Foster striding toward her. Where had they hidden him?

Mamma, Sister, and Winnie holding Peter met her at the door. "Oh, you do look so like a college girl—I can tell by the way you walk!" exclaimed Sister.

"How do college girls walk?"

"Confidently, I guess. I don't know, but I am so

glad to see you. Come on, let's start catching up on everything."

They were pulling her in, seating her in the living room, plying her with questions, and hardly waiting for answers. She kept looking toward the kitchen, then toward the outside door. He must be out walking.

"See our Christmas tree, Judy!" cried Margo.

"Tristmas chee!" echoed Peter, pulling at a colored paper chain.

"Juliana," said Mamma cautiously, "the boys did tell you, didn't they? About Foster not coming?"

"Not coming?" The announcement was too sudden for her to be able to cover her disappointment.

"He had to see about some urgent land business in Florida. He really was very sorry."

"This is for you," said Margo, running to her with a small package.

"Oh, Margo, you shouldn't!" said Winnie.

"It's all right," said Mamma. "I think Juliana needs it now. It's from Foster. He asked me to bring it to you. Go ahead. Open it."

For some reason her fingers shook as she undid the wrappings. She felt everyone's eyes on her, and she kept her own on what she was doing so they wouldn't see the mist of tears that had come. What was so urgent that he couldn't be here for Christmas? What was so terribly important?

When Juliana opened the box and saw the gold watch, her breathing stopped. Not quite believing, she touched it, then turned it over. It was engraved on the back with her name and the date. A small note, folded into a triangle, said, "To the one girl in all the world for me, I give my love and this token of it. I am quite disappointed not to be with you to put it on you myself. But when you receive this, I'll be in hot Florida trying to iron out a land boundary problem. Please forgive me and know that I love you more than anything on earth."

Brother didn't want her to keep the watch. He said it was the next thing to an engagement ring, and surely Mamma wasn't going to agree to that. Mamma said she had been with Foster when he picked it out, thought they had done a rather nice job of selecting it, and if she had not thought Juliana should have it, she certainly wouldn't have carried it all that way in her pocketbook.

"And, Juliana," she said, looking at her with a searching expression, "there is soon coming a time when you must make a decision about that young man. He cannot keep on waiting, though right now he may think he can. A man can only wait so long."

"Mamma! What are you saying? Juliana cannot marry Foster Kirk! Do you want her to be a widow half her life?"

"Brother," said Mamma, looking at him firmly, "it is Juliana's life, and we haven't the right to keep on making her decisions for her. If the two love each other, then they need to be together for as long as they do have."

Brother walked out of the room, muttering something under his breath. Margo climbed into Juliana's lap so the two of them could admire together the beautiful gold watch. "Make the ticks start, Judy. Come on, make the ticks start beating."

CHAPTER 16

Dearest Juliana,

I'm back at Pinedale. The trees along the driveway seemed to reach down to welcome me.

What a precious little picture you made for me. I wish I could have had it to help me through the lonesome holidays, but then it is such a blessing to me now.

Darling, I am so glad you like the watch. If only you could realize that I would give you the world if I could. That is why I didn't come at Christmas—because I was securing an investment for our future. If I hadn't remained in Florida I would have lost half my acreage.

Your mamma and Henry are going to let me buy a little cow from them. She's a good one, Henry says, and I trust him. As you know, dealing with cows is not my strong point!

My Little Girl (thank you for letting me call you mine, even with reservations), let us be honest with each other. Our Lord has taught us to be trusting and trustworthy. Let us never break that bond between us. If another light comes into my life, I will certainly let you know (though I assure you it is highly unlikely). And you must do the same. I say that with a pain of fear in my chest, yet knowing that if you do not love me, I must accept that and go on living the kind of life that I will not be ashamed of when I meet you in heaven.

And now good night, my love. It is very late, but still a whippoorwill is singing, and I will not be alone as I lie awake dreaming of you.

Always,
Foster

Juliana wrote to him faithfully, sitting at her window, struggling to express her feelings. It seemed so easy for Foster to tell her he loved her. Yet, no matter how much she wanted to say it, too, her letters sounded either too bold or too stiff. So she would tear them up and write about The Morgue or the red water or the prospects of Scottish Day to be celebrated in the spring. "He will know when he sees me," she whispered to herself. "He will know that I love him when he sees me."

Clover Hill
January 25, 1923

Dear Juliana,

I hadn't planned to write tonight, but I do want you to know what has happened here, and to assure you that we're all quite safe.

As you know, we have continued to do what we could for the little German peddler. I had taken to giving him eggs and milk whenever he came, he looked so thin and white. Well, I'm very sorry to say that won't be happening any more, for he is dead, attacked on the road by a group of KKK's. It is so hard to believe that there are people right here around us who will do that. And as bad as that is, it isn't really the worst. There was one member of that group who hadn't enough sense to leave the scene and is now behind bars. Blake Davis. The wretched criminals pulled poor Blake into their evil work, and not a one is showing up to speak in his defense. Needless to say, Mrs. Davis is distraught.

Henry is doing what he can to help Blake, and also Foster Kirk is working in his defense.

I wanted you to hear this from us and know that we're safe, rather than to hear it from anywhere else.

Don't worry now. We'll be fine.

Love,
Mamma

Later Mamma sent clippings of the follow-up stories on Blake, who was pronounced not guilty by reason of insanity and sent to the state mental hospital at Milledgeville. To Juliana's relief, she read that the other KKK's were all brought to trial and found guilty. She noticed that the stories were handled well, with honesty and forthrightness, but without the use of scare tactics. It wasn't until she was sliding the clippings back into the envelope, however, that she saw the by-line—Foster Kirk.

Hurriedly she got out paper and pen to express her appreciation. Again she tried to write the all-important words he'd asked her to share whenever she could honestly say them: *I love you.* But the pen would not obey her heart, and the words did not come. She signed her name, then impulsively started a P.S. But again she sat long in thought and finally wrote "Byron and a friend are coming this weekend. We're going to see 'When Knighthood Was In Flower'."

When Foster's letters stopped coming in March, she thought he must have had to make a sudden trip to Florida, or that he was extra busy with an art exhibit in Atlanta. But weeks passed and there was no word from him, though she kept writing him faithfully at Pinedale.

When she got a letter from Grange with a clipping of Foster at the exhibit enclosed, she had to fight the doubts and jealousies that rose inside her. In the picture of Foster and his paintings, Maureen was standing at his elbow. There was no mistaking her profile and the profusion of tight ringlets. He had said to trust, and she was trying. But why didn't he write? True, he wasn't smiling at Maureen in the picture; she could have just happened to be there. But she *was* there, and Juliana knew Maureen—her flirting eyes, her saucy mouth, her possessiveness of what she considered her own.

It became harder and harder for her to keep her mind on French or her other subjects, though she managed to keep her grades up. Miss Gerard was obviously aware that her interest had slipped, and kept giving her little lectures about reaching her full potential, not slacking when things got tough. But French class was right after the morning mail, and she was becoming more and more depressed at the absence of letters in her box. Mamma wrote and said Foster had been to see her and had asked about Juliana as if he hadn't heard from her in a long time. Her heart leapt with hope. Surely there had been a mix-up in the mail. She wrote him again, but still there was no answer.

Early one morning, when she got to the mail room, Juliana saw a letter addressed in a scrawly handwriting lying on The Morgue's desk. When she realized it wasn't to her, the disappointment cut like a knife. Inspecting the letter addressed to Mrs. Morgan, she realized that it wasn't Foster's hand at all, but more like his Aunt De's. Who could Mrs. Morgan know who wrote so nearly like the Kirks? She couldn't read the postmark, so she turned the envelope over to see the return address, but there was none. She was dropping it back on the desk when Mrs. Morgan's door opened, and she burst forth with a guttural, smothered cry. "How dare you molest my mail?"

"I—I thought for a minute it was mine," said Juliana, turning white, and backing away.

"Yours! There is no way you could think my name is yours. They are nothing alike. Young lady, I should report you to the authorities, but I won't—this time. Just take a week's restriction graciously, and get out of my sight this instant."

The week's restriction added to Juliana's misery. She could go nowhere except to the lunchroom and classes. Her friends were very attentive, but even that did not cheer her. Ever one to try to make those around her happy, she tried to play along for their sakes, but they saw right through her act. They had known the jubilant Juliana, and couldn't be fooled. Perhaps the streams, so sluggish all year, might be moving more briskly now that spring was here, but she couldn't go out to see. She missed, too, the fresh air and even the very tame flowers in their precise, unimaginative beds. She almost stopped eating, just nibbling enough so that The Morgue wouldn't take her lunchroom privilege away, too.

At the end of the week Juliana's spirit was so quenched that she could not bring herself to look for her mail. So her roommate offered to check it for her, assuring her again and again that Foster would write soon. In fact, said the roommate, Juliana might just get a whole bundle of letters one day that had been held up in the mail somewhere.

"Juliana Hamilton," spoke Miss Gerard at the end of French one day, "come to my room for a cup of tea."

Juliana was glad that she wasn't on restriction any more. Tea with Miss Gerard would be a bright spot in the midst of so many drab days.

"Juliana, my dear, whatever has happened to you?" asked Miss Gerard as she poured tea and then eased herself primly onto the edge of a delicate chair. "Your grades are not bad, but you have lost your spark. You are doing only what is required, not reaching hungrily for more. You always reminded me of a baby bird crying for more food as fast as the mother could shove it in. Now—now you are just like my other good but boring students. Juliana," she leaned forward and laid a blue-veined hand on her knee, "you have the ability to go far. After one more year of French, if you were back to normal, you would be good—so good that I could recommend you for foreign study. You could study in Paris. Ah! I see some of that old interest returning. I knew you would like that idea!"

"But, Miss Gerard . . ."

"Never before have I been able to recommend anyone for study abroad," said Miss Gerard, standing up and walking around her small finely decorated parlor with her hands clasped in excitement. "If it is money you are worrying about, I can do something about that. If we can't get you a scholarship, I will personally underwrite you. How would you like that?"

"But, Miss Gerard . . ."

"Oh, yes. I know it is a very great deal, but I have saved all my life and have never had anyone to spend it on. It will be as if—as if you are my very own daughter. Yes, that's it!" A spot of bright color in both cheeks betrayed her excitement. "Now, dear, what do you say?" She paused in front of Juliana.

"Miss Gerard, I cannot possibly accept."

"You *cannot?* But why?"

"I am going to be married this summer—I hope."

"Oh, no, no! Marriage! What a waste! No, no, love, think again. You must not throw away all that talent. You must not! Please don't do that to yourself! What about those brothers who have sacrificed for you to come to school? Think how proud they would be. And this young man, too—he would wait."

"Wait? No, I don't think so—not as long as he has waited already."

"But he does not know. You must tell him. Think about it, Juliana. This may be your chance to make your dreams come true."

Her dreams? What dreams? Was this what she'd waited for all these years—to study French in Paris? Her heart froze. Was she to become like Miss Gerard, living in a two-room apartment, teaching others and watching them go into the world, leaving her behind? Or maybe she would become a missionary in a French-speaking country, teaching many children who would never be hers. Her teacup rattled as she set it in the saucer.

"It's very kind of you, Miss Gerard, but I will have to let you know," she said softly.

"Good. You will think about it. The offer is open and will remain so. And in the meantime, do come out of the doldrums. If you are in love, let me tell you: no man is worth all that misery. I should know. I had a fiancé once who said he loved and adored me until, one day, 'The Right Person' walked into his life and snap! it was all over with him. I've learned, Juliana, that there are more important things."

"Thank you very much for the tea," said Juliana. "I must go now."

"But don't forget my offer. Think about it."

Scottish Day was only two weeks before school was out. Byron insisted on bringing a friend to escort Juliana to the various activities—the Maypole dance, Scottish bagpipes concert, and the singing of Scottish songs at midnight. She would have written Foster Kirk to tell him how much she wanted him to be there—not Byron's friend—but there seemed no use. She hadn't heard from Foster now in three months. Instead, she wrote to Grange, telling him all about the exciting day: how pretty the bagpipers' costumes were; what fun it was to dance with Byron's friend who somehow knew how to do the Highland fling, though he'd never done it before; and how cozy it was singing "Loch Lomond" by a bonfire with the stars overhead. She never once mentioned Foster Kirk.

As school drew to a close, Juliana was almost sick with excitement and anticipation. At last she would be returning to Clover Hill. There she could think with a clear mind about Miss Gerard's proposal, and maybe the ache inside of her would ease. Perhaps she would see Grange and he could tell her whether a "new light" had really walked into Foster's life.

CHAPTER 17

IT WAS A LONG, long train ride home from Red Springs. Byron would have come and traveled with Juliana if she could have waited one more day. But she could not possibly stay in that dormitory another day after all her friends left. Besides, maybe it was best to make the trip alone so she could think.

What had she done to make Foster stop writing? She carefully reviewed her letters to him as, almost unnoticed, the fields and foothills slipped past. She had been too careful not to tell him how much she cared. She knew that now. But she had been just as friendly as always, and he had always written back, even though he called her notes "cool and proper."

Maybe it had just finally been more than he could stand, as Mamma had warned. Maybe he had found someone nearer his age. Like Maureen. Henry, Brother, and Byron had worried so about her interest in Foster, because they said she would spend half her life as a widow. Now she knew that it just didn't matter. But Foster himself may have realized how awkward it would be introducing her to his friends in Atlanta and having them, one by one, comment about how she looked like his daughter instead of his wife. Juliana took a small mirror from her pocketbook and studied her reflection. She thought she looked pretty old now, and she could make herself look older if necessary. She could keep her hair up in a bun like Mamma.

It was dark as Henry drove her home from the train station, but he noticed at once the fatigue in her voice. "You sound like all the sparkle has gone out of you. Just wait till you see all the little new calves, and a mess of kittens in the barn, too. And Martha and I have a surprise for you."

"You're going to be—"

"You guessed it. A father! Come October."

"Oh, Henry, how very wonderful! I'm so glad for you both." Then recalling that he had sold his beloved horse, she added, "But I know you miss old John. I'm sorry about that."

"John? John who? Oh, the horse. Pshaw! The old scalawag had to go, that's all. He's on a good farm down toward Commerce. He's all right, and I'm happy. But I—I—won't be completely happy until my little sister is, too," he said gently.

"You mustn't worry about me, Henry. I'm going to be just fine—now I'm home."

But Juliana needed more than calves and kittens to cheer her up now, more than wild tiger lilies in the woods, or the chuckle of Jenkins Branch. The waters of Lorna Doone Falls simply made her cry. There was no joy anywhere.

One night after Henry and Martha were in bed, she poured her heart out to Mamma.

"I don't know what I did to ruin things between Foster and me," she said tearfully. "I wanted to tell him I'd like more than anything to be his wife, but it seemed too important to put on paper, so I decided to wait. Now I don't know what to do."

"It's strange you didn't hear from him," said Mamma with a puzzled frown. "Very strange. Because he came here several times and never once did he seem to have given up on you. Do you suppose . . ."

"Mamma," Juliana interrupted, anticipating the question, "that many letters could not be lost. You know they couldn't. Besides, this study that Miss Gerard wants me to go into . . . well, maybe that's what God wants me to do. Oh, I wish He would just talk out loud and tell me if it's what He wants."

Mamma tied off the threads on a piece of crocheting, smoothed the square in her lap, then looked at Juliana. "Juliana, God doesn't give us life tasks without giving us the desire to do them. He is no cruel taskmaster who holds out good things to us and then snatches them away. He wants you to have joy. How can you give joy to others if you don't have it within you? I don't mean that we can't expect to have hard times, big disappointments, changes in our lives that we can never understand. But the Lord gave you a good brain to learn with and make decisions with. You're just going to have to recognize what you truly want and go after it."

"Mamma, I have no doubt what I want. I want Foster Kirk."

"Anyone who accepts partnership with that man is accepting a calling," said Mamma quite definitely, laying her square on the table.

"But what can I do?" asked Juliana. "He won't answer my letters."

"Tomorrow you're going to Pinedale to see him."

"Mamma! After he hasn't written for weeks?"

"He says *you* didn't write. You go straighten it out. Take the buggy in the morning and go to town and take the train."

"By myself?"

"By yourself."

"You're sure?"

"Much more sure than I was the last time I let you go there alone."

As Juliana started out the next morning, she was tingling with the old feeling of anticipation—of expecting Something Big to happen. However, on the train ride to Clarkesville, she began to be apprehensive. As the train neared the Hill's Crossing stop, she almost decided to go on to Tallulah Falls, but pulled the bell at the last minute. The conductor was quite startled for some reason, and after helping her solicitously down the steps, he questioned her wisdom in coming by herself to such a lonely place.

"You haven't anyone to meet you?" he asked.

"No, it's a surprise," she explained, and waved him on.

It did seem very strange for there to be no Foster

and no Beppo at the stop—strange and very, very lonely. Juliana stood at the crossing as the train puffed away into the distance, and looked across at the big house where Maureen had stayed with her aunt. Wouldn't it be humiliatingly horrible if Foster had married Maureen—or someone—and now here she came barging in, uninvited. But then something Foster had said gave her courage to keep walking. He'd said, "I trust you, and I want you to trust me. No matter how things seem, we must be willing to trust each other."

Well, Mamma was right. She would never forgive herself if she didn't find out exactly how things were. So she walked on between waving Queen Anne's lace and then, in the cool woods, huckleberry bushes loaded with ripe blue berries. She came to a sudden halt at the sight of an old tin pot half full of huckleberries. Since it was at the edge of the path, it seemed that someone had just left it for a minute and would be back soon, might even at this moment be walking toward her. She stood listening, barely breathing, her lips parted slightly in anticipation. The woods seemed vast and filled with footsteps. But it was only the rustle of squirrels, a breeze through the leaves, or just inexplicable cracklings and whisperings of the woods. Finally she walked on—more slowly than before.

She had on the dress Foster had always liked the best, the blue gingham, though it was old and dingy now from Red Springs water. At least the hat was not spoiled. She loosened it now and fanned herself with it as she neared Hilltop. She would see the place he'd talked of building on, the place from which she could see Trey Mountain and Yonah—never-changing, never-moving sentinels.

The sound of a dog barking made her stop. Beppo? She tried to see ahead, but couldn't. The dog was barking quite wildly, she realized now, as she moved cautiously closer. When she saw Beppo, he was bouncing back and forth in a small semicircle, now and then jumping farther backward, scattering leaves as he did. Moving past an invervening tree into the hilltop opening, she gasped audibly at the sight of Foster Kirk, gun raised to shoulder, apparently aiming at Beppo.

"Stop there!" he commanded sharply, never moving the gun barrel an inch or taking his eye from his target.

"Don't shoot!" she cried, but at that very moment he did, and she closed her eyes, unwilling to believe what she'd seen. The explosion was followed by the insistent smell of gunpowder and an unearthly silence, uninterrupted even by the crackle of a leaf or a sigh of wind.

"You can look now, Juliana. I've killed it," said Foster heavily. "I was afraid he was going to get my dog."

She saw it then. A big brown moccasin with its head blown off. Beppo was standing over it, sniffing cautiously at the still-writhing, brown-patterned body.

"It was camouflaged so—I didn't see it," faltered Juliana, her hands shaking now that she knew everything was all right.

"You surely didn't think I was going to shoot my dog!" laughed Foster bitterly as he propped the gun against a tree beside an axe. "He's been my only joy for quite some time now. May I ask why you've come? To collect the picture, I suppose."

"Picture?" she asked stupidly. Then, with understanding, "Oh, no, not the picture! I came to see why you never wrote and answered my many letters."

"Why haven't I written, she says, Beppo boy. You must have a boxful of my letters, Juliana, or would have if you'd saved them."

"I haven't gotten any—since—since March. I wrote and wrote because I wanted you to know . . ." There was a tearful shake in her voice.

"Know what? That you've fallen in love with one of Byron's friends? That you've decided to be a career woman? That you want no more of an old man like me? Well, tell me now. Let me have it straight, and let's get it over and done."

She lifted her head and looked at him, towering above her, his cheeks thinner than usual, his eyes bright, his jaw set hard. "Foster Kirk," she said unsteadily, "I love you with all my heart."

"You—what?"

Encouraged by a leap of hope in his eyes, she put her hands up to his shoulders and said, "I love you with my whole heart." Only she had to finish it against the rough khaki of his shirt where he held her closely with strength and, at the same time, reverent tenderness.

"My little one, oh, my little one! I thought I might never see you again. My life has been so miserable these many months. Juliana, I love you. Nothing else on earth is more important to me."

The questions, all the questions, could wait. Right now, nothing mattered to Juliana except knowing that Foster loved her. Sometime later with Beppo beside them, they walked hand-in-hand down toward the cottage.

"Don't you want your axe—and your gun?"

"I'll get them later. I have more important occupations for my hands right now than killing snakes or trimming underbrush."

"Or picking huckleberries?"

"Yes, that, too," he said, looking down at her with a boyish grin. Then his face grew serious. "You say you haven't had any letters from me since March? And I've had none from you. I wonder who is holding them up."

"I'm afraid I know," she said sadly.

"Not Grange? He would if he could, the sorry rascal, but how could he? He's done his part, telling me every discouraging fact, such as the wonderful time you had on Scottish Day with some lucky guy."

"Oh, he didn't! And I wished so it were you, Foster! Truly I did, but . . ."

"Well, we mustn't worry now that it's over. Only . . . I wish I could get my hands on the person who held up our mail."

"I'm afraid—it must have been Brother and Mrs. Morgan. You have never met such a mean woman in your life, and I'm afraid Brother used her. I'm so ashamed."

He looked down at her, a warm light in his eyes. "I'm so very thankful that you've come to me, love, that I can forgive anyone. Maybe, after all, it helped you make up your mind."

"I knew for sure at Christmas," she said. "I was so horribly disappointed that you didn't come."

He stopped and took both her hands. "Are you really sure now, Juliana? Sure you won't be wondering later if there were some mission you should have gone into? I didn't think I could bear to lose you, but neither can I bear to have you commit your life to being my wife when you'd rather be something else."

Her smile came from the very depths of her eyes, as well as her lips, as she answered confidently, "I'm sure, very sure, Foster, that my mission is with you—to follow those bends in the road with you."

They were in another close embrace, Beppo patiently waiting nearby, when Aunt De's voice caused Juliana to jump back, blushing.

"So—" said Miss Delia Sweet, "my little scheme didn't work. Well, so be it. If I tried that hard to stop it and failed, it must surely be blessed of the Lord."

"Just what did you do?" asked Foster sternly.

"Just a little meddling. It wasn't at all hard to get that Mrs. Morgan to hold up the letters. The woman said you were quite a naughty child, Juliana, and she was very glad to help." Miss Sweet chuckled and reached down to pet Beppo. "Actually made me like you a bit to know you were naughty," she said, sheer mischief shining in her old eyes.

"Aunt De! How dare you!" said Foster, stepping forward.

But Juliana's small, firm hand on his arm stayed him. Looking up earnestly into his face, she said, "What did you say a moment ago? You'd forgive anyone? Did you really mean it?"

He looked down at her and his mustache twitched in a sudden grin. "You little witch!" he said, hugging her tenderly to him.

ABOUT THE AUTHOR

Brenda Knight Graham grew up in the foothills of the Blue Ridge Mountains in northeast Georgia and now lives with her family in the farming district of southwest Georgia. Though her life is centered around her husband's busy veterinary practice and the many activities of her two teen-agers, Brenda finds time to play folk harmonica and speak to civic groups and children's classes and is an active member in her church. She also enjoys making jams and jellies from homegrown fruits.

Though *Juliana of Clover Hill* is fictitious, it is based on the true story of the courtship of Brenda's parents. She became interested in writing the story after completing her first book, *Stone Gables,* which is the story of life at Pinedale as she remembers it in the 1940s and 1950s. Brenda has also written a series of books for children: *The Pattersons at Turkey Hill House, The Pattersons and the Mysterious Airplane,* and *The Pattersons and the Goat Man.*

A Letter To Our Readers

Dear Reader:

Pioneering is an exhilarating experience, filled with opportunities for exploring new frontiers. The Zondervan Corporation is proud to be the first major publisher to launch a series of inspirational romances designed to inspire and uplift as well as to provide wholesome entertainment. In order that we might better contribute to your reading enjoyment, we would appreciate your taking a few minutes to respond to the following questions and return to:

Anne Severance, Editor
Serenade/Saga Books
749 Templeton Drive
Nashville, Tennessee 37205

1. Did you enjoy reading JULIANA OF CLOVER HILL?

   ☐ Very much. I would like to see more books by this author!
   ☐ Moderately
   ☐ I would have enjoyed it more if ______________

2. Where did you purchase this book? ______________

3. What influenced your decision to purchase this book?

   ☐ Cover
   ☐ Title
   ☐ Publicity
   ☐ Back cover copy
   ☐ Friends
   ☐ Other ______________

4. Please rate the following elements (from 1 to 10):

- ☐ Heroine
- ☐ Hero
- ☐ Setting
- ☐ Plot
- ☐ Inspirational theme
- ☐ Secondary characters

5. Which settings do you prefer?

______________________ ______________________

______________________ ______________________

6. What are some inspirational themes you would like to see treated in future Serenade books?

______________________ ______________________

______________________ ______________________

7. Would you be interested in reading other Serenade/Serenata or Serenade/Saga Books?

- ☐ Very interested
- ☐ Moderately interested
- ☐ Not interested

8. Please indicate your age range:

- ☐ Under 18
- ☐ 18–24
- ☐ 25–34
- ☐ 35–45
- ☐ 46–55
- ☐ Over 55

9. Would you be interested in a Serenade book club? If so, please give us your name and address:

Name ______________________________________

Occupation ________________________________

Address ___________________________________

City ____________ State ____________ Zip ________